CARTEL PUBLICATIONS
PRESENTS

SILENCE
OF THE
NINE II
LET THERE BE BLOOD

T. STYLES

NATIONAL BEST SELLING AUTHOR OF *RAUNCHY*

By T. Styles   3

Silence of The Nine II: Let There Be Blood
By T. Styles

PUBLISHER'S NOTE:
This book is a work of fiction. Names, characters, businesses,
Organizations, places, events and incidents are the product
of the
Author's imagination or are used fictionally. Any
resemblance of
Actual persons, living or dead, events, or locales are entirely
coincidental.

Library of Congress Control Number: 2014958176

ISBN 10: 0996099255

ISBN 13: 978-0996099257

Cover Design: Davida Baldwin www.oddballdsgn.com
Editor(s): T. Styles, C. Wash, S Ward
www.thecartelpublications.com
First Edition
Printed in the United States of America

F STY
1910 1057   2-23-18   BLP
Styles, Toy, 1974-

Silence of the nine
SDW

By T. Styles   5

What's Up Fam,

Dayyummnn! This year flew by. Seems like we were just celebrating the holidays in 2013 and now they are back again. We have been working extremely hard to keep good books in your hands and soon good movies and TV shows on your screens so get ready. With what seems like time moving so rapidly, I want to take a second to say something that is deeply on my heart. Please remember, during this holiday season especially, to take time out to spend with your love ones. And during that time spent, make sure you are present. What I'm getting at is, put the phone down, pull your head off of the Internet and really spend precious time. You never know when it may be the last opportunity you get to do it. While you're with your family, remember to **Be Grateful** and keep in mind the people that are no longer with us.

Rest in Peace **Trayvon Martin**, **Mike Brown**, **Eric Garner**, DC Mayor for Life, **Marion Barry** and the LEGEND, **Carlos E. Mavins, Sr.**

Keeping in line with tradition, we want to give respect to a vet or trailblazer paving the way. With that said we would like to recognize:

Oprah Winfrey

Oprah Winfrey is not only a talk show host but she is also a national best selling author. Her latest novel, "Things I Know for Sure" has become one of my favorite non-fiction novels. It's full of stories that Oprah shares with her readers about the things she knows through her life experiences. It is a great book that I wished never ended. Make sure you check it out its perfect nighttime reading.

Aight, I've talked your head off long enough and the book in your hands is tooooo good to wait any longer to get into. I just have one word that describes it, OUTSTANDING! T. has dropped banger after banger this year and "Silence of The Nine 2" will not disappoint! Get to it. I'll catch you in the next novel.

Be Easy!

Charisse "C. Wash" Washington
Vice President
The Cartel Publications
www.thecartelpublications.com
www.facebook.com/publishercwash
Instagram: publishercwash
www.twitter.com/cartelbooks
www.facebook.com/cartelpublications
Follow us on Instagram: Cartelpublications

Dedications

I dedicate this novel to all my Twisted Babies!

Silence of The Nine II: Let There Be Blood

#silenceofthenine2

PROLOGUE
The Future

"If it be dark, how dost thou know 'tis he?"
- William Shakespeare

Leaf's wrists were strapped securely to a sturdy wooden chair, causing the tips of his fingers to run cold. The open wound on his scalp spouted blood before it trickled through the trails of his short mane, eventually spilling down his forehead and pressing through the tiny hairs of his eyelids.

The darkness made it difficult to see his adversaries but he blinked a few times, forcing the red liquid out of the way in an effort to peer within the shadows. "Why you doing this?" he mumbled, the salty metallic taste of his blood heavy on the tip of his tongue. "I don't understand." His body shook uncontrollably although the tone of his voice was somewhat calm.

He was livid.

What did they want with him?

Why had they broken into his home?

Out of the gloominess appeared an elderly woman with an eerie smile. "You really don't know, do you?" She knelt before him and wiped the blood from his vision with the cool but forceful palm of her hand. "You really are an innocent fool."

He swallowed and moved his hands slightly to relieve some of the pressure of the ropes but nothing worked. The restraints would not give no matter what and he was in pure agony. "If I knew what you wanted from me, I wouldn't have asked."

"We need your assistance," the woman said, her smile wider than before. "I wish we didn't but I'm afraid it's come to this moment." She placed a hand on his knee. "There comes a time in life where you have to take a stand. And for me to do that, I need your help."

"So what do you want?"

"Where is Nine Prophet?"

Suddenly the thunder in his head vibrated like sticks to a drum. He was losing so much blood that he was getting dizzy and losing the reality of the moment. "What do you want with her?"

"How fond are you of your wife?" the woman asked.

"Words can't express," he replied, his head drifting backwards.

"How could you not love Nine?" the male collaborator said, his natural voice filled with bass. "She is both alluring and beautiful in the same space. I would never want a woman like that for my own. I'd be too consumed."

"She's a human not a goddess." The woman laughed. "In your adoration, please remember that she is also evil," the woman added as she gazed at Leaf. "If you search your memory I'm sure we don't have to say a lot to convince you of this. You live with her. You see the decisions she makes and you're witnessing firsthand how much power she's accrued." She paused. "What happens when she uses this capacity against you?"

He was in anguish and an unwilling participant in this meeting. All he wanted was to get some help before it was too late. "You beat me," he whispered. "Almost killing me in the process and still I have not received an answer to my question. What do you want?"

"Nothing that you won't be rewarded for in the kingdom of heaven," the woman responded. She stood up and took two steps away without moving deeper into the darkness.

"Rewarded?" he repeated.

"Yes, all are rewarded who stand against evil and tyranny," she said in a compassionate tone.

With all his might, he yelled, "I'm still not hearing what you want!" the gash in his head beat with the pressure of a jackhammer into hard concrete.

Feeling disrespected, she smacked him, forcing his head to jerk to the left. "I'll tell you when the time is right! For now, let me tell you who we are. And what we can do to your life if we are refused." She paused. "We are Disciples. And we bring with us all the wrath that God has bestowed upon us."

CHAPTER ONE
THE PRESENT

"These violent delights have violent ends…"
- William Shakespeare

Leaf rotated away from the warm spot on his bed, to a much chillier side, in search of the roasting temperature of his wife's flesh. With an outstretched hand, he palmed the place she was supposed to be.

But she wasn't there.

Why?

Raising his heavy head, he blinked his eyes open and gazed into the direction she usually slept. Her pillow was without a wrinkle, indicating she'd been gone for some time. He pushed the dark blue 1500 thread-count Egyptian cotton sheets away from his body, and then kicked them on the floor. Slowly he wheeled on his back, opened his eyes wider and stared at the vaulted ceiling.

"Not again," he whispered as he tossed his legs around until the bottoms of his toes nestled comfortably inside a pair of warm brown Ugg slippers at his bedside. "Where are you, Nine?" He realized it was time to forage for his wife within the walls of the mansion.

Again.

Before rising, he took a deep breath, stood up and ambled toward Julius Caesar's crib.

The fourteen-month-old infant was of his bloodline. The infant was his cousin. And yet he was raising the infant as his son.

Using the glow of the night lamp, he lowered his eyes until his gaze fell upon the baby boy whom he'd grown to love as if he were his own. The child's closed eyelids concealed his winsome eyes. "Guess you didn't hear her bounce either," he said before running his index finger down his face.

With the baby safeguarded, he headed toward the part of the house he was sure Nine would be. The same place he met her a little over a year ago. The same place where her blood oozed out of the whip wounds, caused by their grandfather, and spilled onto the floor. Yet it was also the place where she felt most at home.

The basement.

Her prison cell for most of her life.

Leaf, Nine and baby Julius now lived in the Prophet mansion by themselves. Their grandmother, Victoria, died from a broken heart in her room of the mansion a few months after Kerrick passed.

Now in the lower part of the mansion, he walked toward the farthest door within the dark basement. The smell of sawdust and paint was prevalent, since Nine was building something, which she kept private from Leaf.

When he made it to the location, he opened the door carefully. There was nothing inside, not a carpet, not a piece of furniture, not even a picture.

Why she insisted on spending so much time in such a lifeless space he would never understand.

With the doorknob in his hand, he pushed it open. "Cousin," Nine said calmly. "Did I wake you?"

He stopped in place and whispered, "Why are you in the dark? Why do you come here when you can't even see?"

"I can see well, cousin. It is you who is blind," she responded. "Come inside…and close the door behind you."

Reluctantly he did as requested and stepped deeper into what felt like an abyss. There wasn't an open window and the boards covering up the windows had sucked all of the light out of it. "Bae, I can't see you. Let me cut the lights on for a—"

"Do not use your eyes, cousin. Use your instincts and *feel* for me."

Hoping to get things over with quickly so he could get back into bed, he kicked off his slippers and tried to locate her with outstretched hands. He even opened his eyes wider but when he realized they were of no use, he closed them and tried to locate her familiar scent. The lavender oil in her long, soft curly hair. The coconut butter she rubbed over her dark chocolate skin.

Using his nostrils, he inhaled deeply and reconnected with the reason he fell in love with her in the first place. With a new outlook, with each step he was certain he'd find her and he was right. Within a matter of seconds, he reached the other side of the large room and stopped when his big toe nestled between the folds of her vagina.

She giggled and seductively said, "So now you are trying to fuck me with your toe? I knew you were freaky but this is new, even for you."

He opened his eyes despite not being able to see and grinned. Slowly he lowered himself until his hands were upon her knees and then thighs. She was sitting on the floor, back against the wall, and knees in the air.

"You said feel you and I'm doing that," he whispered running his hands over her breasts. "I guess I found you."

"Yes you did, cousin."

"And once again, you in this room naked."

"Is there any other way to be?"

Leaf positioned himself so that his body was against the cool wall next to her. He felt for her hand, located it and pulled it toward his lap. "Nine, can I ask you something?"

"Anything."

"When you gonna stop calling me cousin when I'm your husband?"

She giggled. Nine was the only woman he ever met whose humor and sex appeal were one. Everything she said, everything she did, was done with an ounce of grace and suspicion.

"Why would I stop referring to you as one or the other when they both are the same?" she asked honestly. Taking a deep breath, she leaned her head on his shoulder and drew her knees closer to her chest. "You ever wondered what pleasures grandfather gained when he beat me…ripping into my flesh in this very room?"

"No." He frowned. "Just thinking about it makes me angry." He gripped her hand tighter. "Even at this moment."

"Are you angry because he beat me or because I willingly gave my body to him in exchange for freedom?"

"All of the above."

"It should not bother you so much, cousin. It was not as bad as it seemed."

Taken aback by her response, he asked, "Which part? The sex or the beatings?"

"Would you think I was weird if I said both?"

"So you saying the scars I feel on your back every time we make love are okay with you? That the beatings, the starving…everything was cool?" he asked angrily.

Sensing the irascibility he expressed whenever the subject of Kerrick arose, she said, "Do not get mad, cousin. It is just that sometimes I do not know what I feel. I was taught to hide my emotions for so long." She exhaled. "All I know is that this room comforts me. I am closer to—"

"Fran," he said completing her sentence.

Nine repositioned her body and regained ownership of her hand. "She loved me. She loved me when she had every reason to hate me."

"Is that why you revived Kerrick's vineyard and named the wine produced from it after her? Because she knew how much you loved her, Nine. You don't have to allow them stuffy white people from that winery around our home. We have enough money. You have everything."

"Except Julius' love," she said skipping the subject. "He hates me."

"He doesn't hate you, Nine." He placed his arm around her neck and softly pulled, causing her to press against the side of his body. "He doesn't know you. Spend more time with him, instead of wasting every minute on the Francesca wine venture. Give him time, Nine. He'll learn to love you not as some strange person or even an aunt. But as a son to a mother. There's a reason why you took him into our home after you killed that bitch."

"You mean my sister."

"I mean the woman who tried to kill you, who killed our child in your womb." He paused trying to wipe the hate away. "Despite it all, Julius will learn to love you."

"Yet he has already warmed to you," she responded more sternly. "Without the benefit of coercion. It is as I have always said, cousin. One day he will attempt to kill me and in the moments preceding my death, I will regret not acting first."

Startled by her prophecy and speaking ill of a baby he'd grown to love, he said, "He's a child, bae." He couldn't see her facial expressions but he could feel the fatalistic energy she was exuding gushing out of her pores. "You can't hurt him. Not after you made me love the lil nigga." He paused. "We can't back out of this even if we wanted to. Remember all that time we spent convincing everyone that he was our son, even though they knew you just lost a baby? Don't forget that none of your family members knew that Paige was still alive. If you give him up, they will think that you are giving up your own child. Not a nephew. There's no turning back now."

She giggled. "I am Nine Prophet, cousin. I can do whatever I want at any time I please." She paused. "The sooner you realize it, the better off you will be."

****

The blazing orange sun spilled inside of the massive, sparkling white Prophet dining room via the window. From the view, Nine witnessed her grapevines grow upward, like the natural mane of a beautiful African-American woman. Hanging right below the peacock green bushes were purple droplets of succulent eggplant colored grapes.

Dipped in a silk baby blue gown that melted into the flesh of her body, Nine sat poised in a large brown chair with gold accents that resembled a throne. It was the only chair at the table like it and it was just for her. As she stared out of the floor-to-ceiling window, with her mind on the Francesca wine that would be birthed from the land, she dictated the items of the day to her beautiful young assistant, Banker Troy.

Banker's natural long black hair trickled down the sides of her face and rested at her shoulders. Her brown skin was always touched with very little makeup. She didn't need it. Every so often, she would readjust the red eyeglass frames, absent of medicated lenses, she wore in an effort to appear astute. "Anything else, King?"

"Did my cousin Bethany call? About the wedding?"

Banker flipped through a few sheets on her clipboard and nudged the frames closer to her face with the eraser of her pencil. When she found the message she was looking for, she nodded. "Yes…she said the venue needed an additional one thousand dollars toward the deposit."

"Did she say what for?" She paused with a slight glare. "I have already given a total of seven thousand dollars to that place. How could they want more?"

"She said your aunt Victory wanted to add a few more things."

Nine sighed. "Okay, remind me to write a check and have it delivered by Antonius in the morning." She paused. "Any word about Royal Babies Daycare Center?" she asked nervously. "Did they accept Julius?"

Via Banker, Nine had been trying to get into the prestigious daycare center since she found out about its existence. It was an elite facility where, if Julius were accepted, he would have access to a top-notch education. Her nephew, dressed as her son, would be in the company of the children of politicians and movie stars who had homes around the Prophet mansion in Aristocrat Hills.

But there was one problem; she knew that her family's name was known by some of the locals within her affluent town. One hint of incest or controversy and Julius would not have the tutelage befitting a king. So she had Banker represent herself as if she were Julius' mother until he was able to acquire a space within the center. Once that achievement was gained, Nine would step up and win them over with her personality, she was certain.

"I haven't heard anything yet," she sighed realizing Nine despised disappointment.

"Stay on top of them, Banker. And get in contact with Antonius today and tell me what he needs from me," Nine instructed as she cut into a blood red orange, causing the cerise-colored juice to spill onto her silk gown. "His voice sounded frantic so if it is an emergency, reach me immediately wherever I am."

When Nine wiped at the red liquid, causing the juice to span wider on her clothes, Banker jumped up, plucked a few napkins out of the sterling silver holder on the table and lapped at the liquid on Nine's gown.

"Mrs. Prophet, you look as if you've murdered yourself."

Nine observed the girl with wider eyes, appearing to be in a daze. Confused at her choice of words. "Murdered myself?"

Instead of responding, Banker continued pressing the soggy napkin against Nine's body, rubbing over her firm breasts more times than need be. It was as if by touching her, she was hoping to gain one ounce of the poise, the power and the sexuality Nine possessed.

Due to the pressure she was exerting, Nine's nipples rose beneath the expensive silk fabric. Banker was so caught up in polishing Nine that she hadn't realized that she placed herself in a trance.

"Banker," Nine said softly after being amused by her assistant's sudden change of personality for long enough. She'd never seen her that way and she'd never been molested by her either. "Are you okay?"

Banker blinked a few times, realized she overstepped her boundaries, dropped the drenched napkins and pushed her frames closer to her face. "Uh…yes…I'm fine," she smiled awkwardly. Picking up her pencil, she asked, "If I reach Antonius and learn that it is not an emergency, what should I tell him?"

By T. Styles   19

"That I will contact him at my earliest convenience," she said easing the citrus fruit into her mouth, before running her pink tongue over her fingertips, arousing Banker even more. "Any other messages?"

"Yes," Banker said flipping through the notes for the day. "Someone by the name of Bambi Kennedy contacted you. She told me to warn you about upcoming danger. And that all of the bosses need to band together or your banks will be in jeopardy."

Nine was quite aware of the message Bambi Kennedy tried to encrypt to her assistant. The Kennedys were at war with the Russians and as one of the bosses, Bambi was doing all she could to solicit help from local drug lords on the east coast. And since Nine controlled one of the most powerful brands at the present, which included one thousand soldiers, it was only fitting that Bambi solicit her help.

"Tell her that right now, the war with the Russians is a Kennedy problem. But when or if that changes in the future, she may count on Prophet support."

Banker wrote down the message diligently. "Anything else, King?"

"Are there any other messages?"

"I think that's—"

When there was a knock at the front door Banker scooped up her paperwork and said, "I'll be in the office." She was frantic as she tried to disappear. "Please let me know if you need anything else."

Nine nodded her head and grinned as she watched the girl hustle into the walls of the house. Since she first started working for Nine six months earlier, she noticed that she had a shy disposition. She met Banker through an organization for the wealthy who needed help with private matters. She won Nine over with her professionalism and how well she picked up on Nine's needs in advance.

When Nine's housekeeper Elizabeth James, an elderly white woman, scurried past Nine and opened the door, Nine waltzed toward it. Elizabeth held the door open with her pale wrinkled hand, which was trembling due to having acquired Parkinson's Disease.

"Liz, you are dismissed," Nine said. Nine placed her warm hand on the doorknob and the eyes of the woman, who stood on the outside, widened as if she'd seen a ghost.

Nine focused on the woman. "Who are you?" she asked firmly.

As she waited on a response, Nine took a moment to observe the woman's chiseled features. She wore a yellow and gold head wrap and matching dashiki, and she stood with the air of an ancient African queen. "I am Chipo Chunghwa."

"And what are you doing here?"

"I am looking for Kerrick Khumalo." The woman appeared mesmerized by Nine. Her eyes rolled over her face, the bloody stain on her gown, down to her feet and even her hands.

Nine, although usually graceful, upon hearing her grandfather's name, clasped her hands in front of her and toyed with her fingertips. "Khumalo?" She never heard Khumalo associated with him before.

Chipo shook her head in recognition of her error. "I'm sorry." She grinned. "You probably know him as Kerrick Prophet."

Nine sighed. "I am sorry, ma'am, but Kerrick has been dead for well over a year now." When Nine glanced down at the blood-colored stain on her gown she felt bad for not wearing a robe.

Perhaps that is why the woman stares so hard, she thought. *I look a sight.*

Chipo seemed genuinely surprised upon hearing the tragic news about Kerrick and yet it explained why she had not heard from him. She stumbled backwards and for some reason, Nine immediately assisted her, giving her the respect she would have Fran.

Who was this woman?

And why did she move her so?

"Please come in," Nine said helping her to the luxurious sofa. When the woman was seated, Nine took her place in front of her on a cozy recliner. "Excuse my appearance. A piece of fruit ruined my state. I am usually more put together than this."

"Your appearance has not been touched one morsel. In fact, it's...you...are you his granddaughter?" she asked, her words running together.

"I am," Nine said crossing her legs and resting her hands on her knees.

"But you look so much like my daughter...my only child," she responded as each word followed heavy breaths.

"And she is?"

"Thandi Khumalo. Kerrick's first wife."

****

Nine strolled in the backyard along the pathway of her vineyard, arm in arm with Johnny Gates. Although she remembered their meeting, her mind was on Chipo and the relationship she had with her grandfather.

Chipo enlightened Nine greatly on she and Kerrick's bond. Although evil to some, his honor and code were strong in some aspects of his life. Especially as it pertained to his first wife.

The moment Kerrick became a wealthy man, he sent millions a year to Chipo, which she used to rebuild her village in Africa as well as the schools. He never forgave himself for Thandi's death and dedicated his life to expressing to her mother how sorry he felt.

At first, Chipo ignored his checks, never cashing a one. Besides, she was angry at how he left her to mend her daughter's body, which was brutally torn apart due to his career of stealing babies and selling them to men who believed raping virgins would rid them of HIV. An after kidnapping the wrong child, as payback, Thandi was murdered and Kerrick fled to America for fear he'd be next.

Beside herself with grief, Chipo cursed Kerrick. Condemning him to a world of sadness so that his karma would be repaid in full in this lifetime. And when she saw Nine, who resembled her daughter, she recognized the power she possessed. She knew she was powerful, but it wasn't until that moment that she learned how much. Not only had Kerrick's last days been hell, he had fallen in love with his granddaughter in order to be reconnected to the wife he never got over.

In a sense, it was suicide by love.

"Where's your mind, beautiful?" Johnny Gates asked.

"Here with you. Where else would it be?"

"How come I don't believe you?"

"I am not sure," she exhaled before inhaling the sweet odor from her vineyard. "Because nothing else could be truer."

"Why am I not allowed in your home anymore? When you and I are such good friends?"

"You know the answer, Sir Gates."

"I wouldn't ask if I did."

"Because you are *my* associate and yet Leaf does not want you in our home. I enjoy your company, Sir Gates, but I have to respect my husband. He comes first, always."

Johnny was a fifty-eight-year-old man who had been in the drug business longer than he cared to admit. Although he was prosperous, he was prudent about his purchases and finances. Outside of his home, his driver and his Rolls Royce, he kept most purchases discreet and low.

His father, Billy Gates, was the biggest dealer Houston had ever seen. But he had a penchant for pussy and even indulged himself with his best friend's wife, which caused him to be hung by his neck for all his men to see.

So Johnny, who was twenty at the time, took the money his father stashed at the house, along with his knowledge of the business, to Baltimore City for a new start. There he met Abraham, Kerrick's old boss, and supplied him heroin using his father's connect.

Business was good. That was, until Abraham's neck was slit at his ten-year-old son's football game. At first, no one knew he was dead. His lifeless stare was taken as a lack of enthusiasm since his kid's team was losing. But when the game was over and his son walked into the bleachers and touched him, Abraham's body fell on top of him. Then everyone had become aware that Kerrick Prophet murdered ~~him~~.

The reason for the hit was known to most. Kerrick gained the trust of a Miami drug cartel and they supplied him with pure cocaine. Abraham refused to use Kerrick's product and paid for this slight with his life. Although Kerrick still didn't supply Baltimore—because Johnny Gates, who is a made man, was next in charge—Kerrick's reputation for ruthlessness was legendary.

Which was the sole reason Gates never trusted him.

Kerrick was going to kill Gates too but the men he trusted, Mox, Riley and Jameson, warned him against it. They said that if he made a move without authorization, his entire family would be annihilated. Kerrick was going to take his chances and kill him anyway until Gates made a classy move first.

Gates invited Kerrick to a luxurious cigar bar outside of Baltimore. And over expensive smokes and whisky, he respectfully declined his offer to use his product. His tactfulness was the only reason Kerrick allowed him to live. Everybody else who bucked against his system was buried along with their close family members and friends.

After awhile, Gates grew interesting to Kerrick. He was a man who got everything he wanted but he couldn't get Gates to relent. Gates was a challenge. The more he said no, the more Kerrick trusted him as a man of his word, which was why he invited him to his home. Gates had proven that he wasn't a man of circumstance, but a man of integrity, something that he couldn't say for himself.

Although very different, in one way they were alike. They had big families. Gates with his three daughters—a set of twins, Dymond and Berry, and a seventeen-year-old daughter, Chloe.

Once peaceful, things between the Gates and the Prophets took a turn for the worse when Chloe and Leaf met in high school. This was way before he knew Nine existed. Although sex together was explosive, Leaf wanted nothing more than a friends-with-benefits scenario. Chloe on the other hand felt differently. Feeling rejected, she pulled a gun on him in front of the school in an attempt to take his life. Unfortunately for her, Leaf defended himself and in the end, Chloe lay dead in front of her school.

Changing the direction of both the Gates' and Prophets' worlds.

Instead of Gates accepting that the matter was self-defense, and realizing all was fair in love and war, he instructed two men to enter the Prophet mansion to kill everyone...especially Leaf.

His plan looked foolproof except he hadn't expected that Kerrick had been raising Nine, a natural born killer, under the floors of his mansion. With her bare hands, she brought them both down, thereby winning her grandfather's respect, love and admiration.

Knowing that revenge was a doubled-headed sword, under Nine's command, the Prophet family descended upon the Gates property. Gates had to pay for his disrespect and yet Kerrick was unwilling to kill him. After all, there was still money to be made.

Although Nine was not present the night of the approach on Gates, her family threatened Gates into submission. He was either going to get on the right side of business or else lose everyone he loved. And to showcase an act of Kerrick's villainous spirit, they murdered another one of Gates' daughters, Dymond Gates.

To say Gates was devastated was an understatement. He dreamed of the night he would feel the flesh of Kerrick's throat against his fingertips but he was beaten to the punch. It was Nine who murdered her own grandfather with the worst weapon.

One he adored.

Nature.

For days, Kerrick breathed in the poisonous odor of an aconite plant until he died in his own home. It was done out of revenge. Because for every day of her life he beat her with a whip in an effort to kill her slowly and still he failed.

Gates took a strong liking to the young and powerful Nine and decided to do business with her.

"Your vineyard is beautiful," Gates said as he looked down into Nine's beautiful face. "But a bet is a bet." He ran his finger along her cheek. "So when are you going to give in to me?"

She chuckled lightly. "Why do it to yourself, Sir Gates?" she asked seductively. "When you know you will never have me. When you know that I belong to Leaf and Leaf alone."

He tried to hide the disgust he had in his heart for Leaf. But the right side of his cheek puffed before flattening again. "A married woman, even one as powerful as you, must still pay what she owes. It is how you attain and maintain respect."

She nodded. "This is true, Sir Gates." She stopped walking, stepped in front of him and lowered down halfway. "I always pay my debts."

Raising the edge of her dress slightly, she removed her gold silk panties. Slowly she raised them and placed them under his nose. The dampness of the seat brushed against his left nostril. He inhaled deeply. "You smell as sweet as I imagined." She giggled and walked arm in arm with him again before he stuffed the panties in his pocket.

"Tell me something, how did you know that the boxer you sold me would win the championship? He looked so meek and for some reason, I did not think it possible. I figured he needed at least a good six months to build stamina."

"As you know already, I'm out of the boxing business. Which is why I referred him to you."

"And I thank you deeply," she winked.

"I know, my beauty." He exhaled. "But there is no need for thanks." He paused. "When I was younger I was a boxer. Went as far as I could before the lure of pure white cocaine called me. Now, well, now despite being out of the game, I still have the eye to recognize a champion." He stopped and stepped in front of her. "And I recognize that in you, King Nine. From the moment I saw your face."

"I must admit, I was hoping you would lose."

"You treasure my painting by Antoinette Bateau that much?" He chuckled. "I never knew you were into young whores who were decapitated by their pimps."

"Neither did I until I saw the work of art on your wall," she laughed. "Tell me, Sir Gates, how powerful do you think the human psyche is?" she asked seriously. "How much do you think a human can endure?"

He exhaled and they sat on a stone bench marked Francesca, which faced the vineyard. "Let's see, when I first saw you, you were naked. Standing in front of the refrigerator. The skin on your back was shredded and I figured life would always be hard for you. And now here I stand, face to face with one of the most powerful women in the world. If that's not an example of the strength of the human psyche, I don't know what is."

She blushed. "You are too good to me. In another life, I would love to see the future we could create. As husband and wife." She looped her arm through his and leaned on his shoulder. "But now, well, now, we do well in coke and money and we will have to respect that."

"You and your new drug connect have made me very rich."

"Then why not let me buy you out of Baltimore. I am willing to pay any price you want. Just name it."

"I guess I enjoy the business, Nine. What will I do without moving coke? Can you understand that?"

"But you said you were ready to retire. So let me help you with that. The beaches of Aruba are calling your name."

He laughed. "The funny thing is if you want to overthrow me, you probably could."

"That is not true," she exhaled. "Your connections with your associates have been in place longer than I have been alive. They would never work with me if you do not bless the union and step down."

"Then I guess you'll have to be with me a little while longer." He looked down at her. "You have a problem with that?"

"Sadly, I do not," she giggled. "It would probably be my pleasure." She gazed at her vineyard.

As they continued their conversation, Leaf looked out of the window, brewing with anger. He could never understand why she insisted on being in a personal relationship with Gates. But Leaf had plans for him and he couldn't wait to put them into action.

If done right, his wife would be none the wiser.

CHAPTER TWO

"A dammed saint, an honorable villain!"
- **William Shakespeare**

Alice sat on the floor, with her knees pressed against her chest as she peered at her feuding cousins within her Aunt Victory's house. Twenty white adult cats crawled around, leaving behind long strands of their white hair. It was on everything. The furniture, the carpets, the curtains and even the walls. When one cat tried to nestle next to her, she shoed it away with a stiff fist. She wasn't there for cuddles, fucks or hugs. Her visit marked a more important reason.

Samantha and Bethany were in a heated argument and her temples throbbed painfully. She wasn't sure if it was because of the yelling or her light brown hair being snatched back too tight in a ponytail, forcing the corners of her eyes to reach upwards.

She scratched her naturally blushed cheeks, her nails pushing against the raised scars on her face, compliments of the torture that Nine subjected her to for sixteen weeks, almost a year ago. The abuse included rape by strange men and beatings like she never imagined were possible. Despite that lesson, Alice still harbored ill will for Nine.

As her cousins continued to fight, she pulled her knees closer to her body, causing her salmon-colored dress with tiny white bows embedded throughout, to spill to the sides of her thighs, in turn revealing her hairy vagina and pink center.

Panties were a nuisance that Alice Prophet learned to live without.

Although twenty-two, she had a knack for dressing like an innocent child, church girl gear included. No matter what she wore, her spirit remained dark and those who came within her presence only needed five seconds to feel something was off with her. Something was evil in her soul. Something iniquitous that even she couldn't put a finger on.

What was eating Alice Prophet?

Suddenly the fight kicked up to another level as their voices rose. To outsiders the disagreement might seem outlandish, taboo and even ungodly. But the Prophets, they were raised in this type of environment and in their world everything made sense.

At the end of the day two sisters, Samantha and Bethany, were fighting over the love of one man. Their brother, Noel Prophet. Since the Prophet way was to breed amongst themselves, thereby preserving the bloodline and keeping the money within the family, Prophet men were scarce and a hot commodity. At present, there were a total of four living Prophet men. They were Blake, his son Noel, Justin and his son Leaf.

So if Bethany and Samantha were going to remain true to the rituals bestowed upon them by Kerrick, then they would have to marry one of the four, or find a man worthy of mixing bloodlines. But Blake was their father, Justin was disgusted by incest and Leaf belonged to Nine. The only man left was Noel and they were willing to kill each other for his love.

Although the argument appeared to be about Samantha wearing Bethany's clothing without permission, in actuality it was about Samantha not being allowed to participate in the upcoming illegal Prophet wedding.

The day on which Noel would be wed to his sister.

"Oh, girls, what's going on now?" Victory yelled waddling into the living room, wiping her fingertips on a yellow hand towel. Her large frame jiggled as she moved briskly toward her daughters, her light skin reddening with each step. The black slacks she wore were covered with so much cat hair they looked white. "Prophet women are to be seen, not heard." She proceeded to separate them by forcefully tearing them apart at their wrists. "Now stop this mess this instant! If Nine were to see you like this she'd surely shorten our monthly stipends. You see what has happened to your Aunt Marina and Uncle Joshua!"

Bethany rolled her eyes. "Mama, Nine is not like that."

Victory frowned. "Is that why you two used to be close and now your relationship has suffered?"

"It's not like that. I have a life with Noel and she is running the family business so we don't have time to kick it. But I never lost respect for her."

Give me a break, Alice thought, as she wanted to throw up in her mouth.

"What this is about is Samantha! I'm tired of her coming into my room and stealing my shit!" Bethany was a smaller, younger and much more beautiful version of her mother but their features were still similar.

"What are you claiming she did now?"

"I came into my bedroom earlier and saw my new Dior blouse missing so I approached her about it. And she had it on, claiming it was hers. Why must she continue to go through my shit?"

"I told you it's mine!" Samantha yelled in her face, her teeth exposed in a snarl. Nothing like her sister in the looks department, her thin lips stretched as her unattractive face contorted in outrage. "You're just jealous because Noel and I went to breakfast today without you!" She crossed her arms over her chest. "Tell mama the truth! You're trying to separate us because you're afraid you'll lose him!"

"I wasn't angry, Samantha. But since we're talking about it, I know you keep inviting him out to keep him from me. But he's already made his decision. He wants me, not you!"

"Girls, please stop arguing." She looked down at her niece. "Oh, Alice, please close your legs. Your girl's package is showing."

For spite, Alice opened her legs wider and Victory rolled her eyes.

Victory focused back on her daughters. "Both of you need to go to your rooms," she demanded. "And while you're up there I want one of you to check on Isabel. God only knows what crazy ghost will take your sister's mind hostage today."

"I can't wait until Noel and I are out of here, then I won't have to be subject to the bullshit," Bethany said stomping away.

When the young adults marched toward their rooms, Alice got up and followed Victory to the living room. "So what are you buying them for a wedding gift?" She clutched her hands behind her back.

Victory's eyes lit up. "A car," she boasted. "A new Mercedes. I want to give it to her before she and Samantha take that flight to Florida to pick up the wedding dress from the designer."

"You have the money saved for the car?"

"No but I'm sure Nine will give it to me," she said confidently. "My daddy bought me a car when I married and I want her to have the same." She began to daydream.

"Have you given any more thought to what's really important? That doesn't include this wedding?"

Victory plopped down on the sofa. "Not now, Alice." She tossed the hand towel beside her. "Can't you see that it's the wrong time? Weren't you paying attention to the status of my family? My girls are in love with the same man and it's tearing us apart."

Alice paced her Aunt Victory's luxurious living room. The wood scent of the logs burning in the fireplace filled the space as her soiled bare feet pressed against the thick cream carpet fibers. "War is around the corner, Aunt Victory!" She stopped. "A crazy woman is running the family fortune and I'm going to prove it!"

"Then do you. Why must you bother me?"

"I hate that you don't care!"

Victory poured herself a glass of wine from the open bottle on the end table. "Why do you think I don't care?" Victory giggled as the stem of the wine glass sat between her fingers. "Because I don't jump on the bandwagon to condemn Nine just because you say so?"

Alice stopped pacing and stood in front of her aunt, stuffing her fists into the curves of her hips. She gave her a cold hard glare because in her opinion, she was weak.

Victory's golden hair was pulled back into a tight bun; her light skin remained reddened due to the heat of the liquor coursing through her veins.

"No," she dropped to her knees and kissed her aunt's leg before placing the side of her face upon it. She plucked a few cat hairs off her upper lip. "You are stupid because you don't see that she is not a real Prophet...like us...even her skin color says it is so. You are stupid because grandfather, in his illness, made the decision of cutting us out of the will, when he loved us so much just months before he died, and still you refuse to act." She looked up at her. "Think about it, Auntie. Who was fairer to grandfather than I? And yet I was shut out of the fortune entirely."

Victory stroked her niece's hair lovingly. She was always so uptight and as her favorite, she wished she'd calm down.

"Even if you believe that grandfather was in the right frame of mind when he left a slave who lived in the basement the family fortune, are you dumb enough to believe he left her everything without her manipulation? Shunning even his own children?"

"My father never really liked me," she admitted. "Although he was quite fond of you." She sighed. "I think he disapproved of my weight, or my love for money."

"And there's nothing wrong with it, Auntie. You have a right to desire what's yours."

Victory sipped her wine. "You're right. It does seem odd that he chose Nine. But if he put her in charge of the family fortune, then he must've felt there was a reason." She downed the rest of the wine and sat the glass on the expensive table. "Besides, Nine is fair, Alice. Even your mother gets a small cut. You're the only one who has been left out of the money altogether. Maybe you're just jealous."

She raised her head. "Fuck is that supposed to mean?"

"Oh, Alice, mind your tongue! It' so dirty." She shook her head. "For whatever reason, she hates you. And only you and her know why. I'm not sure what went down in daddy's house between you and Nine but I do know it's your business, not mine. And I'd appreciate if you leave me out of it."

"It's my problem now, Aunt Victory, but it will be yours soon. Besides, don't pin her picture next to Mother Theresa just yet. You'll see her true colors any day now. Mark my words."

"You should be careful, Alice. Your actions could end fatally."

Alice crawled away from her aunt. She sat against the wall with her knees drawn to her chest. "She hasn't killed me because in her sick mind, I remind her of home, in the dungeon, before the power. Before she lost Fran. But soon that will all change because she hates me."

"Why does she hate you so much? What happened in daddy's house? And why won't you tell me?"

"Nothing happened," she lied, refusing to tell the tales of how she and her late fiancé Hector raped Nine for sport.

Hector met his fate a long time ago in a house fire. Fingers pointed to Nine, although nothing could be proven.

"All I know is that one day she will make a decision that I no longer should be alive," she continued. "But when that happens, who's next? You? Your children? Your husband?" She placed her hand over her heart. "We are real Prophets! Not that black bitch! So let's put an end to the charades now!"

"Put an end to what charades, my dear cousin?" Nine asked entering Victory's home. As with every place she went, members of the Legion were present. They included Antonius, her most trusted soldier, and two other men. "Mine?"

Alice gazed at Nine before looking at Victory. "Hold up, you gave this chick keys?"

"She has keys to all of the Prophet homes. Including your mother's," Victory said shamefully, too greedy to stand on her own two feet and demand some semblance of privacy.

Alice stood up and stepped toward Nine. When she was within a breath's distance, she moved her lips toward her earlobe. She wanted to be sure that only she and Nine could hear her next words. "You look real powerful now, Nine. But I remember a time where I was more powerful than you. If I try hard enough, I can even feel your wet tongue licking my dirty feet for a bite of chicken." She giggled softly and lowered her voice even more. "So scared you pissed your pajamas." She raised her head and looked directly into Nine's eyes. "So you see, cousin, no matter how much power you wield today, you'll never be bigger than me tomorrow. I will always own you."

Nine giggled and twisted a long strand of hair from Alice's ponytail. "You are like a video game to me, Alice. One I enjoy playing. Very much. But when I am done…when you no longer amuse me…I will throw you away and get another, one with better levels and challenges. And there will not be a thing you can do outside of bowing at my feet where you belong." She kissed her on the cheek. "Still think you are more powerful than me?"

Alice wiped her kiss off and stomped away.

****

Isabel's Room

Although she was moving, Alice's entire body was tense as she walked down the hallway. Her fists, her forehead and even her stomach were rolled into huge knots. She felt as if her cousin had gotten the better of her. How dare Nine speak to her so brashly, as if she were a genuine Prophet? She couldn't wait until she brought that tight smile off of her perfect black face.

After being irritated beyond belief, Alice decided it was time to relieve some of the traction on her brain. So she moved toward her favorite room inside of her Aunt Victory's house. The one belonging to her eccentric cousin.

When she made it to the door, she twisted the gold knob with the eagle accents around the perimeter. Once open, she peeked inside.

It was Isabel Prophet's room.

For all intents and purposes, she was labeled the craziest of the Prophets. And considering the members of the family were immersed in dysfunction, that was saying a lot.

Alice blinked a few times and the corners of her mouth still managed to stay in a frown, until she saw Isabel's face. Slowly the curves of her lips raised and presented a smile.

Nine was now the furthest thing from her mind.

Isabel was sitting in the corner of her beautiful purple and gold accented room. Soft curls sprouted from the edges of her long braids, which ran down her back. The baby blue gown she was wearing was long enough to cover her entire body.

She was sitting in the classic Prophet pose, on the floor, knees drawn into her chest, revealing the pinkness of her center. Although there was never a meeting about how to perch like a Prophet, the position seemed to provide the Prophet women with a sense of calm.

Upon seeing her cousin, Alice walked fully into the bedroom, closing and locking the door behind her. "Get the fuck over here," Alice demanded. At the moment, she was reminded of a time when she was able to boss Nine around, and her pussy moistened with thoughts of yesterday.

Like the old Nine, on her hands and knees, Isabel crawled toward her. Once at her feet, slowly she rose until both cousins were face to face. Eye to eye. Exchanging breaths.

Isabel's stare was flat, revealing no emotion.

What is going on behind your eyes? Alice thought.

Not even when Isabel raised her hand and slapped Alice in the face so hard her neck snapped to the side, did Isabel's expression change. At the moment, she was without a soul and still something was there. Deep inside, behind the chest cavity, beneath the organs, where it could remain protected from those who meant to take more from her than she could give.

The blow of the slap forced Alice to her knees. As if she were given silent orders, she raised the bottom of Isabel's gown. Placing her mouth against the center of her pussy, she could smell a strong pissy odor that drove her sexually insane.

The nastier the coition the better, to hear Alice tell it.

Isabel looked down, placed the bottom of her foot on the top of Alice's head and said, "Lick it clean. Leave not a taste of my juices behind." In this room, behind that door, Isabel was in charge. The combination of the poor attempt to downplay her own beauty and the acting out of her wild mind, all made her fascinating.

And yet she was a sexual deviant.

Any nasty, vile and depraved feat imaginable, she'd done it all. Most times against her will. Having her body used for pleasure by her father and his friends since the age of six had caused her to run cold when it came to sexual acts with men. She viewed them as mundane rituals done to please men enough to leave her alone. After some time, when they stretched out the walls of her womb, her mind began to speak out via loud loops of crazy colors. Each demanding that she react violently at a whim.

Despite being raped in the past, it had been a long time since a man touched her flesh. Since the event she decided would be the last. He was Richard Toddling, a friend of her father who enjoyed her so much he stopped coming over to keep her father company, and instead hit it back to Isabel's room.

Richard was always atrocious. He smelled of alcohol, old meat and body gas and he never bathed. For years, she wondered how he was able to live with himself, let alone step into the space of another human being.

Reaching under the pillow her head rested against, as he pumped into her body, she removed the blade and severed his penis from his groin. Blood splashed over everything visible as he rolled off of her and slammed against the floor. His un-humanlike wail caused Victory and Blake to fly into the room. The moment they ogled the bloody sight, they rushed him out of the house and he was taken to a small private hospital where Kerrick gave a lot of donations. A hospital that kept Prophet secrets when they were beyond his patchwork.

Kerrick was devastated after learning what happened to his grandchild and how the man lost his penis. Incest was one thing, allowing an outsider to rape his grandchildren was another. So as always, he managed to make the controversy go away. No one ever heard from Richard again and no one ever touched Isabel either.

But every now and again, when the colors were too loud or too bright, she gave herself pleasure by flicking her clitoris in an effort to ease the crazies.

It always worked.

Although beautiful to behold, Isabel was a whimsical teen with an imagination as vivid as that of a child with a box of new Crayons. As a result, through self-induced orgasms, she developed a way to escape within the walls of her mind. Ironically, she experienced bouts of clarity most of the time.

Most said she would never give her body to a man without severe pain and after what she'd been through, Isabel did not disagree.

When Alice failed to lick her pussy correctly, Isabel slapped her roughly in the face. "Do it properly, Alice. Like I told you. I bore easily and today my mind is a mess. I wouldn't want to hurt you. On purpose or in pleasure."

Alice was in ecstasy.

****

After sex, Alice was perched in the corner of Isabel's room. Her back was against the cool wall while Isabel's head lay nestled face up in the center of her lap. One of her cousin's braids was squeezed between Alice's fingertips as she thought about her trials and tribulations. "Tell me something, Isabel, do you adore Nine Prophet?" she asked softly. "Have you fallen under her spell like grandfather and the others?"

"I have to confess, I don't know her like I should," Isabel sighed. "One moment she didn't exist and the next she suddenly appeared, as queen to the Prophet throne." Isabel grinned. "As if she came from the ground. Like she'd always been there but we didn't see her until that moment." Isabel looked up at the ceiling, still grinning. The idea of rising from the depths was fascinating. "You have to admit, someone with the power to control grandfather is worth knowing."

Upon hearing her foolish statement, Alice felt her blood brewing inside. "I disagree. Anybody like that should be watched carefully, not revered." She paused. "Besides, she's crazy, you know?"

"And so am I," Isabel reminded her. "Don't let the long moments of sanity fool you. I know who and what I am."

"Whatever," Alice continued, waving the air. "In all of your craziness, at least you're an authentic member of this family. She is not even a real Prophet, Isabel. The sooner you and the rest of the family realize that, the better off we'll all be."

"Tell me, Alice, what makes a *real* Prophet?"

"One who is born with fair skin and one who is of grandfather and grandmother's bloodline."

Isabel rose and leaned against the wall next to Alice. "Doesn't she come from Aunt Kelly and Uncle Avery?"

"If you ask me, that's still up for debate. While it is true that it appears as if she were born from a Prophet, why is her skin so dark? Why does she look nothing like the rest of us?"

Isabel shrugged. "Oh, Alice, try to rest your mind. You act loonier than me at times. There are so many things going on in this family. So many secrets and so many lies. Let's not fight amongst each other for grandfather's throne."

"What are you talking about?" she asked seriously, with the taste of her cousin still on her tongue.

"Let's see, you and I fuck like it is normal. Our family breeds amongst each other, each feeling that it's okay because it's the Prophet way. And every one of us is mentally ruined because of it. I'm just the only one who expresses it sometimes."

"You don't know what you're talking about, Isabel."

"Of course I do." She grabbed Alice's hand. "What difference does it make if Nine has dark skin? Have you forgotten that she shares the same complexion as grandfather?"

Silence.

Staring into space, she asked, "Why do you think he loved her more than me?"

"But he did love you, Alice. Just differently."

"But he never took me into his bed like he did Nine."

"Because your body was spoiled, like mine, by your father. Nine was without another man until grandfather took her. At least that's what I heard." Isabel giggled a little to lighten the mood. "You are my favorite cousin. You stay with me whether I'm sane or insane. But I must be honest about my perception."

Alice turned her head to wait for her statement.

"You aren't really concerned with her dark skin. You are more concerned with who holds the power. And since she does, you covet it badly...don't you?"

Silence. Alice looked away.

"You don't have to say a word, Alice. Besides, you and I know that I'll probably forget this entire conversation a few days from now. So let me do my best to make myself clearer." She paused. "Don't go against Nine Prophet. Don't throw a stone at the one who sits on the throne. You will not win."

Alice turned her head back to look into Isabel's eyes. She spit on Isabel's hand and flashed her a cold, evil smile. "I smelled your pussy a few moments ago, Isabel. You stink of rotten fish! Next time, wash thoroughly, or I won't be so quick to pleasure you!"

****

Alice and Isabel walked through the front door of the luxury condominium where she lived with her parents Marina and Joshua Saint. When Alice opened the front door and smelled the sweet stank odor associated with smoking crack cocaine, her stomach churned.

"So I guess Auntie is home," Isabel said shaking her head. She placed her fingers over her nose for fear of getting high and going crazier than she already was.

Embarrassed, Alice said, "Just help me pack some clothes to stay over your house. I don't want to be here longer than I have to."

As they walked down the hallway and bent the corner toward Alice's room, they stopped short when they saw Marina sitting in the lotus position smoking a crack pipe. At one point, Marina was one of the most beautiful Prophet sisters, which was how she landed Joshua Saint, a wealthy real estate mogul in his day. She received the blessing to marry outside of the family from Kerrick but now she was only a shell of her former self.

Her tall, lanky body was so emaciated that you could see the formation of her skeletal system beneath her pale skin. Most of her hair shed a long time ago and what was left in its place were a few straggly ends that could be blown away with a soft gust of wind.

Marina may have fallen off in the looks department but she wasn't the only one to go downhill. When the real estate market crashed, Joshua lost all of his investments and could never get a foot back into the industry because of his drug habit.

Now he was the director of a non-profit agency for children, and no one was aware of his addiction.

Marina, upon seeing her daughter and niece, inhaled the smoke deeper into her lungs and exhaled. With a wide smile, she said, "If you girls knew how I felt right now you wouldn't be judging me." She raised it in their direction. "You'd be joining me."

Alice rolled her eyes and stomped toward her room, the pungent odor of the drugs perfumed her clothing and skin. When she made it to the last door down the hallway she pushed the door open. In a hurry, Alice dropped to her knees, slid out a pink and black suitcase from under her bed and tossed it on top of the mattress.

While she busied herself, Isabel leaned up against the wall and took a moment to look around. The room was much smaller than the one she had when they owned a mansion, before Nine reduced Marina's monthly allowance to one percent, due to her drug habit and disdain for Alice, but everything was neat. There wasn't a stitch of clothing or furniture out of place in the pink and white room. Not even a piece of hair or lint. It looked as upright and honest as the sweet clothing Alice wore to conceal her inner demons.

"I don't get you," Isabel said leaning against the wall, before sliding down and pulling her knees toward her chest.

"What's there to get?

Isabel looked around again. "You don't strike me as someone who would be as orderly as you are."

Alice opened the suitcase and walked to her dresser to remove several sets of folded panties, pajamas and church dresses. "What does that mean, Izzy?"

"I don't know," she shrugged. "You're just…different."

"Well you see order and I see a room built for a pygmy. I'm not supposed to live like this, Isabel. Before Nine cut me out of the fortune and reduced my mother's take, we had a home! A real home not this piece of shit and it's not fair! Grandfather didn't mean for me to live like this! I know he didn't. He would probably roll over in his grave if he saw what Nine has done to me!"

Her constant ranting about grandfather and Nine irritated everyone, especially Isabel. Alice's problems in Isabel's opinion paled in comparison to her own.

"At least you have your sanity," Isabel said softly. "I would give anything to be able to stay in the present. To prevent my mind from going to strange places that don't exist. Every time I go somewhere, every time I come in contact with another human being, I fear I'll leave my mind and not remember who or what I am."

"With the way my life has been going, I would kill for your reality, Isabel."

"Why is that?"

"Because at least you get to stay in your body and have an escape," Alice said in a heavy whisper. "This world is overrated. You have what I want and I have what you want. I guess that's why we work."

When the front door closed, Alice smiled and turned to face her bedroom door. She looked as if she were a child waiting on a big surprise on Christmas day. Every second that passed, it looked as if she were about to explode, as if the anticipation was killing her and as Isabel saw her tense body, she figured it was.

It took a few seconds but eventually the man of the hour appeared in the doorway. Her father. Joshua Saint. "Look at my sweet, innocent little girl," he said licking his lips before taking his gaze up and down her body. "I see you're wearing the dress daddy loves."

Although Alice was twenty-two, Joshua preferred to look upon her as a child, which was why she dressed like a juvenile instead of the grown woman she actually was.

"Hi, daddy," she said grinning. "I almost missed you. But I'm so glad I didn't. I'm leaving to stay with Aunt Victory for a little while."

"Well I'm glad I'm here, sweetheart." He rushed into the room and planted his arms around her before giving her a soft peck on the lips.

Unlike Isabel's father who raped Isabel, Joshua used a slyer form of molestation to win his daughter's heart. He seduced her into a sexual relationship for most of her life and she was gone, unable to accept the reality that her father was nothing more than a vile pedophile.

Alice saw things another way.

In her mind, they were in love but couldn't be together because others wouldn't accept their adoration for each other. His manipulations poisoned her mind, causing her to compete with Marina, thereby destroying the bond a mother and daughter should share.

While they greeted each other, Isabel sat on the floor and looked up at them with detestation. She hated him. Hated everything he represented but especially the sly smile he exposed whenever he was in Alice's presence.

And whenever he looked at her.

Isabel might have been deemed touched, but she was far smarter than the average Prophet and she knew some things were off limits. And that included men sleeping with their own daughters.

Even grandfather didn't go for that, she thought. *Despite the relationship he had with Nine.*

"So you walk right past me without saying anything just to come see this bitch?" Marina asked, walking into the doorway and leaning on the frame. Her eyes were as glossy as marbles, consumed with ego and void of life. "I've been waiting for you to get home all day, Joshua. What about me? Don't I deserve at least a hello?"

Joshua released the hold he had on Alice, turned around and looked over at his wife. Sensing a fight, Isabel stood up, grabbed a few items out of the closet and threw them in the suitcase before closing it in a hurry.

"You were getting high, Marina," he said through clenched teeth. "Without me, at that." He paused throwing his arms up in the air before dropping them by his sides. "Besides, ain't nothing wrong with a man greeting his daughter if he wants to."

"I was getting high without you because I bought it myself. Remember the rule? You made it! If you don't put in on it, you can't get none."

Joshua's teeth began to grind. "Forget all that," he responded waving her off. Joshua was a lot of things but he never used profanity. "Like I said, ain't nothing wrong with a man spending time with his daughter. If you got a problem with it so be it!"

"It is a problem if a man's daughter wants to fuck him!"

Their relationship went on under her nose for years and now, with the drugs in her system, she forgot about her part in the situation. How she allowed his molestation to happen, and pretended not to know, for fear that he would leave and she would be the only Prophet sister alone.

Isabel pulled the suitcase off the bed, grabbed Alice's hand and whispered, "Let's go. Don't let her do this to you."

But Alice was unresponsive. Her mother had her undivided attention and she couldn't hear a thing but her evil words replaying over and over in her mind.

It is if she wants to fuck him.

"He's my daddy. And you just…"

In seconds flat, Marina was in front of her daughter and wiping her dirty nails down her face, pulling flesh along with her stroke. Alice, too afraid to fight, protected herself by balling up tightly and running in the corner. Blood trickled down her face and she was about to rip her up again when Joshua grabbed her from behind and tore her away. "What is wrong with you? She's your daughter!"

"She ain't none of my daughter! She's just some bitch who wants my husband! She can't have him!" She looked at Alice with a contorted glare. "Do you hear me? You can't have him!"

Not wanting to be around the drama, which would cause her mind to go awry, Isabel grabbed Alice's hand, pulling her out of the room and toward the door. Once they were outside of the condominium, she dug into Alice's jean pocket and removed the car keys. Alice was in a zombie-like state and Isabel felt sorry for her.

She wasn't big bad Alice Prophet anymore.

She was a child. A product of dysfunction.

She softly lifted Alice's hand and placed the car keys in the middle of her palm. "Let's go home, Alice. You don't have to stay here."

Alice turned around and looked up at the condominium. "You believe in reincarnation?"

"I don't know," she shrugged. "Never gave much thought to it before I guess."

"You think if I die and come back, I'll get a mother who loves me?" She turned to Isabel and a single tear rolled from her eye. "Oh, Isabel, I would give up everything if that were true. Everything."

CHAPTER THREE

"Take him and cut him out in little stars."
- William Shakespeare

Mo Wright lay on the damp bed, his long leg dangling off the edge as he gripped the back of sixteen-year-old Sheena's neck tightly. Stabbing the center of her warm vagina repeatedly with his penis, he was in ecstasy at how deeply he'd fallen for the youngin'.

Their rendezvous wasn't supposed to be that way. It wasn't supposed to be that powerful. He knew she was much younger than he was and that her father would kill him, but he allowed himself to fall deeper for someone he was not supposed to have.

When he felt himself about to surrender to her strokes by cumming deeply inside of her womb, he released the hold on her throat and smacked her in the face, forcing a lustful smile to span the corners of her mouth.

Oh how she enjoyed pain by him, because at least his attention remained on her. Where it belonged.

He was trying to regain control over a relationship where he had none. She was in charge and if she took herself away from him, he would be lost.

"I love you, Sheena," he moaned. "Even though we shouldn't be together. I know it's fucked up because Antonius will never understand how much I love you."

"Let nothing stop us from enjoying this moment, Mo. Not age. Not circumstances and not my father."

He was about to release into her when suddenly the front door leading into the polluted motel room came crashing down. Mo Wright, forever quick with his whistle, was too sedated that night and he received a bullet to his palm as he reached for the .45 on the table next to the bed.

Twenty-five armed men crawled into a space built for two. And despite the crowdedness, the soldiers split down the middle, making way for Nine to stroll calmly through.

Sheena may have been causing a commotion by screaming and yelling at the top of her adolescent lungs, but it didn't stop Nine's soldiers, called the Legion, from speckling Mo Wright with red laser lights. In case he got gymnastic, they would push so many holes through his body he would be liquefied in seconds.

"Get her out of here," Nine demanded as Sheena was hoisted off of the bed kicking and screaming the entire way. Removing the long Valentino scarf from around her neck, Nine tossed it to one of the soldiers. "And place this over her naked body. I do not want her father to see her that way."

When she was gone Mo Wright yelled, "Who the fuck are ya'll?" Blood spouted from his hand like a water fountain but he remained still on the bed. He knew he was outnumbered and outwitted.

Antonius sought help and found his missing daughter by way of Nine Prophet.

Instead of responding verbally, Nine strolled over to him, each step slow and calculating. The suspense was killing Mo because he couldn't read her expression. Once next to the bed, she snatched an unused condom off the table. Then she kicked off her designer shoes and placed one foot on the mattress followed by the other. Standing over Mo Wright, she raised her dress and reduced her height so that she was straddling his body.

Her men knew what was going on without words even though Mo didn't. Sliding the condom on his dick, Nine raised her waist slightly before she slid onto his shaft, engulfing his thickness in the process. She bucked one time and her pussy gripped his rod as if she was shaking his hand firmly.

When he was turned on, despite his life being in danger, she said, "This is how it feels to fuck a woman who understands the weight of her decisions." She paused. "You just slept with a naive child." She grabbed the gun from the back of her jacket and pointed at his face. "And now you know the difference." She fired into his forehead, killing him instantly.

Seated in the backseat of a gold Maybach with the word "Prophet" splayed on the license plates, Nine spoke to her most loyal lieutenant whom she named Antonius. His born name was Ian Greiner but as with all of the men in her Legion, she gave him a Roman name fitting of their union with her organization.

He and the nobles were the only members in the Legion who were aware that the Prophets were incestuous people.

"I thought I lost her," Antonius said as he melted into the leather seat while staring out of the window as his daughter was being placed in the back of a black Mercedes truck against her will. He hadn't seen or heard from her in weeks and now she would be taken home.

Now she was safe.

He looked at Nine. "And once again, you came through for me." He stroked his smooth goatee that decorated his dark skin. He was stunning.

Nine gazed outside at Mo Wright's body, which was being placed in the back of a van with no windows. When the corpse was inside, she focused back on her most trusted soldier. "We are family, Antonius. You claim you know this but then you thank me for frivolous things. I reward loyalty with loyalty. So why would I not make time for you? Make time to find your daughter when it was clear that her absence troubled you?"

He chuckled. "How do you do that?"

"Do what?"

"Make everyone in your camp feel as if they're the only one?"

She exhaled. "If you lived the life I have, beneath the floors, then you would truly see that every person, every experience, no matter how wretched, is still precious. I have a violent way about me, Antonius, and I cannot deny it. But I revere every moment as if it would be my last."

She touched his thigh innocently but that didn't stop his manhood from stiffening with lust. There was something about a powerful woman that drove him mad and yet he realized he could never possess her.

Not in the way he wanted anyway.

"What can I do to repay you?"

She exhaled, overwhelmed by all of her unresolved issues. "Actually I have two things." She remembered the smug look on Alice's face over her aunt's house. "My cousin Alice is untrustworthy and I might want her slain."

"Just say the word."

"Give me some days. I need to be around my family when the murder happens so that they will not suspect me." She giggled to herself. "Even though with the power I possess, I could be dead and still be capable of murder."

He laughed. "Anything else?"

"Yes," she said growing serious. "I got word that one of our own has been failing in the math classes. He does not see the need for the education part of my operation and yet I cannot dismiss him. If I do, I am afraid I will lose him to the streets."

"Maybe you should, Nine. You can't change or help everybody."

"If I truly believed that, then I would not be here in front of you now." She paused. "The odds were against me and yet someone believed in me, Antonius." She exhaled. "Her name was Fran."

"Why him?"

"His father was Jameson, one of the nobles who died of cancer some months back." Nine's gaze fell upon nothingness. "He was one of my grandfather's closest friends. I was there in his final hours and he always spoke about his one regret in life."

"What was that?"

"Not having a stronger hand in his son's life. He begged me to see to it that he gets right and I want to honor that because I could see in his eyes that his soul would not rest without that peace." She paused. "He was much more honorable than my grandfather, although they shared similar traits. Even down to them both being from Africa." She sighed. "Keep an eye on Galileo. He is young but he is also talented. If we can get him where he needs to be, eventually, he will be one ounce as good as you are."

"That's a tall order."

She laughed. "Yes it is, but no doubt still true."

"For you, I will do anything." He looked into her eyes and she felt his respect, love and lust all at once.

"I know, Antonius. And that is why you are my favorite."

****

The Coliseum Wine Manufacturers

Nine held the sample bottle designed for her upcoming venture with The Coliseum Wine Manufacturers in the palm of her hand. She was savvy in the relationship she was building with the corporation and although Nine never had an ounce of formal training, she was smarter than the average accountant.

She knew numbers well and, as a result, was able to funnel drug money into legit businesses to hide the family's illegal entitics. On the surface, she was a millionaire with billionaire potential. She paid taxes and was always on time and the government was none the wiser.

In her opinion, the drug business should be run like any other corporation. Smart and by the book. In fact, Nine didn't have one stack of money in her house or on her person, believing that if the police raided the mansion they would be sadly disappointed. There were no drugs allowed on her property and although her soldiers practiced shooting on the acres of land covering Aristocrat Hills, she dressed the self-run school up as a program to give at-risk men a chance at a good life, as opposed to headquarters for a drug operation.

With the deal she was forging with the wine manufacturers, she would be placing fifty percent of the money into the venture. It wasn't because she desired to invest her own capital. This was done because the winery didn't have complete faith in the new entrepreneur. They figured if she wanted to prove herself, she would have to assume half the risk by supplying half of the money, and the use of her vineyard.

Nine needed their assistance because although she was wealthy, they had distribution and she wanted her product everywhere fine wines were sold. For the sake of seeing Francesca on shelves, she was willing to do anything.

There wasn't a day that went by where she didn't think about Fran, to a point of obsession.

"So what do you think?" Mr. Berkeley asked sitting across from her in his office. Approving the bottle design was the first step of the plan. There were many more to make before the grapes from her vineyard were selected and she penned a check for production.

Nine ran her fingertips over the purple label with the gold letters that read *Francesca*. "It's beautiful," she said looking at him and then at the bottle again. She was in love and her cheeks rose toward the sky. "Simply beautiful. Oh, how I wish she could see it."

When she gazed to her left to get Leaf's opinion, she saw he was in a trance while typing on his phone. Who was he speaking with that had him so stuck? "Cousin, what do you think?"

Silence.

Leaf continued to text, unaware of Nine's question. A small attempt to be nosey was made on her part, but she couldn't decipher the words due to the dark screen cover on his phone. She felt foolish anyway for prying and decided to stop trying. It didn't stop the jealousy from brewing inside of her chest. She placed her hand on his and said, "Cousin, do you like the design? Mr. Berkley is waiting and you are being rude."

Realizing she was speaking to him, Leaf suspiciously stuffed his phone into his pocket and looked into her eyes before staring at the sample. In his opinion, if you'd seen one wine bottle you'd seen them all. He wasn't interested in making wine or anything else for that matter. All he wanted to do was be with his wife and their son. "Uh…it's nice, bae. Do you like it?"

She pinched him out of view of Mr. Berkeley for calling her bae. How she wished he remembered the script while out in public. They were supposed to be cousins, not lovers. Even though in Prophet-land, both were one in the same.

"Yes, I like it," he responded clearing his throat.

"Well, great!" Mr. Berkley said slapping his pale hands together before rubbing them briskly. "I'll make the design team aware and I'll let you know when the bottle is scheduled for production." He paused before getting serious. "But I do have to remind you of one thing. This is a Catholic company. I know it's hard to believe since we are in the wine business but it's still true." He lowered his brow and looked at her intently. "We cannot be affiliated with any bad publicity from our partners. Now, you and your cousin seem like reputable people, but can I count on you to stay out of the public eye in any negative way? And that includes your family as well."

Nine looked at Leaf. It felt as if a bowling ball rolled down her chest cavity and landed in her stomach. Not only was she sitting next to her cousin, the love of her life, but also she was illegally married to him. A Prophet, in the public's eyes, was anything but respectable and upstanding so she was forced to be deceitful.

"Of course," she said crossing her legs. She refused to look at Leaf because she could feel him staring a hole into the side of her face. He hated counterfeit people and fake shit and this entire performance was paramount. "You are doing business with respectable people," she said. "That, I can assure you of."

He stood up and shook their hands. "Great!" He smiled brightly. "Okay, I'll be in contact with you in the next few weeks. And congratulations on Francesca. This is bound to be an exciting venture!"

When he left his office Leaf wanted to give her an earful about the pinch but Nine called her aunt and avoided a confrontation.

For the moment anyway.

There was no way she was allowing anything or anybody to get in the way of the venture so she had to meet with her family and get things in order. They needed a firm plan and she would give them direction. "Aunt Victory, this is Nine. I need an audience with you."

"Of course, honey! Actually, you called at the right time. I'm planning a soiree of sorts over my house in a few days. You know, to celebrate Noel and Bethany's upcoming nuptials. All of the Prophets will be here," she giggled. "Can I make a place set for you and Leaf?"

Leaf hated, among other things, being around his father's side of the family, but she spoke for him anyway. Besides, she would use the opportunity to make her expectations of the family clear. "Yes, you can count on us to attend. And, Auntie, please make sure everyone is present. I have a few things to discuss that cannot wait."

"Of course, niece. Every person with Prophet blood pumping in their veins will be here. Don't you worry about a thing."

****

Leaf was lying face up on his bed smoking a blunt, thinking about his life. Once a player, now he was in love with a woman who was too unpredictable.

Was his heart safe with her?

Nine's need to fit into a society that didn't embrace her kind was weighing on their relationship. And it was also pushing him further away.

As he inhaled the smoke, suddenly the bedroom door cracked open and in the doorway Nine stood in her favorite outfit...nothing. She had just taken a bath so the smell of Dove soap permeated the air as the puddles of water rolled

By T. Styles　　53

down her chocolate frame, sprinkling gently against the floor.

"Grandfather is asleep and I was wondering if you have any of them honey buns on you," she joked.

He smiled and suppressed his need to laugh loudly due to her role-play. This was the thing that he loved about her. The part no one got to see when they were alone. When she was herself. "Yeah, I got one of them joints for you," he said as he winked. "Come on over here so I can give it to you."

Nine glided toward him and he rolled over and put out the blunt. She pulled the sheet and comforter off his body and smiled at his thickness. "What do I have to do to get it?"

"Use your imagination," he responded. "I'm sure you can come up with something."

Standing at the foot of the bed, she licked her pink pouty lips and then lowered her head to suck each of his toes. Knowing how much he loved that shit, she was not surprised when she glanced up and saw his dick so hard it pulsated to its own beat. While she tended to one foot, the other experienced a soft rub as her titty brushed against it.

After teasing him enough, she crawled on top of him like a lioness. Before sitting on his throne, she pumped her fingers in and out of her pussy before pulling them out and licking them. They sparkled with her wetness. With the show officially over, she spread her strawberry pink center and fucked him slowly before going wild.

Leaf appreciated her diligence but in the bedroom, he was captain. So he flipped her over so that her stomach pressed into the expensive sheets and her ass rose. Now she could do nothing but submit to his will. He pushed her legs wider and rammed his dick into her slushiness.

He glanced down at her flesh. There was something ugly and beautiful about the scars on her back that led to her plump ass. Could a woman with such a history of violence be tamed?

Being sucked into her softness, he snaked his hands beneath her body and pawed her breasts. The image of his light-skinned ass rising and falling into her dark body was picture perfect, worthy of framing.

It was beautiful.

They fucked for two hours straight before he plunged into her one last time, all of their energy gone.

When they were done, he rolled over and looked at her. Nine gazed at him and ran her hand through his curly hair. "The way you love me..."

Silence.

"I just...I cannot explain."

"Try."

"I can see it in your eyes and in the way you hold me. What did I do to deserve your love?"

"You have the blueprint to that, bae. So you tell me."

"Are you excited about the wine?" Nine asked happily. Just thinking about the idea gave her tingles. "This will be the thing that makes the Prophet family legitimate. If we do this right, we will never have to sell dope again."

"We don't have to sell dope now," he said dryly and clearly uninterested.

"Are you happy, cousin?" She paused touching his face. "Like I am?"

Her smile was intoxicating and for the moment, he wanted to ease her worries. "Of course."

She grinned as if she just hit the lottery. "Is there anything I can do to show you how much I love you?" She paused. "Anything at all."

"Nothing, Nine. Except you being here for this family and not worrying so much about things that do not matter."

"Being home is a given." She waved at the air. "But is there anything else?"

Silence.

"Yes. Abandon the name Prophet and take my last name. Lincoln."

She sighed and rolled over on her back. His persistence on an issue she would not budge on was annoying at best. "Why must you do this every time we get together? Every time we make love and you pleasure me? Whether my last name is Lincoln or not, I am still a Prophet. We both are."

"So the answer is no?"

Silence.

He rolled over on his back as they both ogled the ceiling. "Do you have that honey bun for real?"

Although a little annoyed, he reached over, opened his drawer and handed it to her. She ripped at the plastic, and took a big bite. Even to this day, with all the money she possessed, it was her favorite treat. Smiling with a mouthful of the pastry, she said, "I cannot believe you really have it. I thought you were playing."

"I got everything you need." He looked into her eyes. "And one day you'll realize it."

CHAPTER FOUR

"Told by an idiot, full of sound and fury."
- William Shakespeare

Banker sat in the driver's seat of her Lexus outside of her home with her cell phone pressed against her ear. The other hand was stuffed inside of the lips of her pussy as she flipped her clit several times to the sound of her boyfriend's low and seductive voice. She was supposed to be going to work but was sidetracked by his need to be freaky.

"I'm doing it now, Galileo," she breathed heavily. "I'm playing with myself. What else you want me to do?"

"Is it wet, baby?" he whispered harshly. On the other side of the phone, miles away, he stroked his thick dick, getting off heavily on the whisper of her voice.

He should've been studying for the calculus class all Legion members had to attend, but he couldn't care less about Nine's rules or procedures. To hear him tell it, he knew enough about life and worked with her solely to move dope and get money.

Not an education.

It was interesting to him that Nine kept him around despite his disrespect for authority. He went as far as to start dating her assistant, despite Nine being unaware. If she were, the repercussions would be great. Banker met Galileo, whose birth name was Gene Hatchett, at the Legion training facility the day she dropped something off for Antonius. The two had been inseparable ever since.

"I'm so wet it feels like I pissed on myself," she answered truthfully. "I can't wait for you to—"

Banker's voice was trapped in the center of her chest when she looked out of the window and saw Alice's beautiful but scratched face staring at her. Alice motioned for her to roll the window down and in a trance, Banker complied. "Yes?" She pulled her soggy fingers from between her legs, wiped them on her jeans and put the phone on her other ear.

"Hang up the phone," Alice said calmly. "I know you know who I am…and we must talk. Now."

Banker complied immediately. "G, I gotta call you back." "Something wrong?"

"I don't think so." She pushed the button to end the call before he disputed further.

"May I sit inside of your car? This is kind of private."

She nodded yes.

Alice strutted to the passenger side, slid inside and adjusted the air conditioning system to her comfort level without asking. "Tell me, Banker, how does Nine treat you?"

"I don't know what you mean." She shifted a little in her seat, trying to button her jeans.

"You speak English, right?"

Banker frowned. "Yeah…"

"Then what part of my sentence structure don't you understand?"

Silence.

"I don't think about it a lot. I guess she treats me alright." She shrugged. She took a few moments to recall the conversation she had with her earlier about Royal Babies Daycare Center. All Nine wanted to know was did she hear anything about Julius' entrance and once again she said no. This angered Nine although she tried to remain calm as she gave her orders.

"So out of your entire employment history with Nine, she never once treated you wrong?"

"A few times she tried to seduce me but I was hip to that shit." She looked Alice over, trying to feel what she really wanted from her. What she really wanted her to say. "Why do you ask?"

"Seduce you how?"

"You know how some women be wanting you to fuck them even though you don't go that way. That's what Nine does. Like one day, I was preparing her itinerary and some red juice from an orange spilled on her gown. I was taking notes when all of a sudden she told me to get it off and not to leave a drop behind. But the juice was on her breasts and she made me rub her titties to clean it off."

Alice could tell that Banker was either attracted to Nine, ashamed, or jealous. Either way, she knew she could use her intricacies for her malicious advantage. "Nine is very sly, Banker. And I know I've only seen you around and—"

Her voice rose. "I was told not to speak to you if I ever met you," Banker blurted out. "I could get fired with you just being here. So I really must know something." She paused. "What do you want with me?"

"I'm not surprised at your reaction. Nine will do all she can to stop people from being around me and hearing the truth. But you're not like some of the other dumb mothafuckas are you? I have a feeling that you move to the beat of your own heart."

"Fuck no," she said puffing out her chest. "I hate how she makes me call her King and how the soldiers be so far up her ass they can see her thoughts. She ain't even all that pretty if you ask me," she continued to lie. "Not pretty like people be trying to make her out anyway. Just ordinary. Plain old ordinary."

"Wow, Banker, you're smarter than I thought," she said playing on her cockiness. "That's why I wanted to meet you and introduce myself personally." She paused. "First, I have to know, do you believe that I'm dangerous? Have her worthless warnings gotten to you?"

Banker looked her over. "Uh…not really."

"Well you shouldn't. The only thing I want to do is look out for you. And if we're going to be good friends, it's important for you to believe me."

Banker's naive smile spread across her face before disappearing as if it never existed. "Cut the shit, Alice Prophet," she said through clenched teeth. "The only thing I want to hear is what do you want me to do and what's in it for me. So save all of the other shit and start talking dollars and cents."

CHAPTER FIVE

"Where love is great, the littlest doubts are fear."
- William Shakespeare

Leaf and Noel strolled into a bar, grabbed two stools and sat down. Their presence said power, marked by the six men who hung in the background to protect them with their lives. After ordering drinks from the bartender, they checked out the football game on the huge TV screen on the wall, the Dallas Cowboys versus the Washington Redskins.

"I appreciate you going with me to order my tux, man," Noel said glancing at the Cowboys making a run for a touchdown. "I'm not going to lie, unless I'm at a Prophet business meeting with Nine, I don't do the dress up thing much. So I appreciate your help. Your wife doesn't allow the casual dress type of outfit."

Leaf laughed and shook his head. "Yeah, my wife can get a little extra when it comes to her rules. She grew up on them Roman books and shit. Royalty and honor is all she talks about. But she means well."

When his phone buzzed and he saw a text message from Nine, he rolled his eyes when he saw its contents. *The Coliseum is having a press conference for us tomorrow to discuss the venture. Wear your suit and tie. I'm so excited!*

Irritated, Leaf stuffed his phone back into his pocket.

"You aight?" Noel asked placing a hand on Leaf's back.

"As right as rain."

Noel nodded. "I ain't got no problem with dressing up, by the way," he said as he tossed his cognac back. "My wardrobe has gotten refined since she took over the business." He flagged the bartender for two more drinks. "So have you given any more thought to being in my wedding?"

Leaf shook his head in slight irritation because they'd had this conversation before. He dug in his pocket, took out his cell phone and looked at the screen. He was expecting an important text any minute now. "Come on, man. I fucks with you but I can't get down with the Prophet politics. I already told you that."

Noel frowned. "Fuck that 'sposed to mean?"

"Sisters marrying brothers and shit." He laughed. "No offense, man, but that's ya'll thing not mine."

"Says the man who's married to his cousin," he chuckled.

"It isn't the same thing."

"Keep it real, Leaf, you a Prophet too. The worst job you can do in life is making a profession of shunning your own people. Fucked up or not, at the end of the day, we're all you got."

"I'm not a Prophet," Leaf said pointing to himself. "My last name's Lincoln and when I met my wife, I didn't know she was my cousin. My father, who I don't fuck with no more, didn't tell me. By the time I found out, I was already in love."

"So why didn't you end the relationship?"

Leaf shook his head, unwilling to recognize the similarities. "Like I said, it ain't the same thing."

Noel laughed. "When are you going to realize that there's something in the Prophet blood that makes us favor our own? Whether your last name is Lincoln or not, if you came from Kerrick and Victoria you're a Prophet. Look at your complexion. Yellow skin and curly hair. Intelligence. All Prophet traits."

"Drop it," Leaf said, uneasy with the topic of discussion.

"What's up with your father?" Noel asked, only having met his uncle briefly when Kerrick was alive.

Leaf moved uneasily. "He hasn't talked to me since me and Nine got together."

"Damn, that's fucked up." He scratched his jaw.

"I tried to kick it with him but he made his position clear so what could I do?" he shrugged. "Anyway, I got too much on my mind to be thinking about that type shit."

"Wouldn't happen to be about Gates would it?"

Leaf's eyebrows rose. "How you know?"

"Because his old ass is always hanging around. Don't make no sense if you ask me. The nobles already said she should keep him at a distance."

"I understand that she's playing the nigga close to get Baltimore out from up under him, but the way she going about it is foul. Inviting him outside of our crib and shit like that."

"He be in your house?"

Leaf laughed him out. "Come on, Noel, the nigga not crazy enough to come in my house."

"So why don't you tell her to stop seeing him?" He paused. "On second thought, she probably wouldn't listen anyway. How do you control a woman with power?"

Leaf positioned himself so that he could clearly see his cousin's eyes. "I don't know what you got going on with your sister-slash-wife on that side of town, but anything I ask my wife to do, she does." He pointed a stiff finger into the bar. "No questions asked."

"So what's the problem?"

"I don't activate that type of power unless I must. I want her to do what's right because she wants to, not because I told her. On the block ya'll salute her but at home I'm king."

Noel nodded. "Fair enough, King, but I will say this, never allow a man with affluence to spend too much time around your wife. You don't ever want to test that type situation. You may lose."

****

Galileo and Banker

Galileo lay face down on his bed as he pumped into Banker's mouth as if it were a pussy. As he rose in and out of her throat, he pawed one side of her head like a basketball. There was no sense of how his girlfriend felt or even if she could breathe. He was going to reach his orgasm. That was the bottom line.

Banker lay face up, naked, with her knees pointed to the ceiling as she tried to remain calm and not die. Thick lines of vomit rested on the sides of her cheeks and mixed into her hair. On several occasions, she couldn't breathe and choked and not one time did he stop.

After a few more pumps, when she felt a thick salty substance run down her throat, instead of being disgusted she was relieved.

It was finally over.

"Go wipe your face and bring me a washcloth," he said as he lay on his back, grabbed the remote and turned the TV on. He placed one hand behind his head, crossed his legs and was glued into the football game. He had already forgotten about how good she made him feel even though he was still sore.

When she came back into the room, she handed him the rag and looked over at him. She was horny and her clitoris throbbed and she wanted him to offer her relief. "So you not gonna hook me up?" She sat on the bed, with her bare ass on his pillow and back against the headboard. She covered her body with the damp sheet.

Galileo wiped his dick and tossed the washcloth on the floor. "I'll fuck you later," he said preferring to see men in tight pants play football instead of his naked girlfriend.

In a weak voice, she said, "Come on, baby, I want you to kiss it for me."

He frowned. "Nah, shawty." He paused. "I don't feel like all that shit right now."

Defeated, Banker sighed and rolled a blunt to ease her mind. If she couldn't cum, at least she could get high. When she ran the fire over the edge of the blunt, and it was good and hard, she handed it to him. He snatched it without saying thank you. "Nine is in my business too much lately," he said as he lit the weed and inhaled before handing it to her. "I can't take it no more."

"So what you want to do?"

"First, are you sure you can do that thing you was talking about?" he asked looking over at her seriously.

"With getting into her bank accounts?"

"Yeah."

"I know I can," she said confidently. "Why?"

"Because we gonna need money if we kill her like we talked about."

"That's kinda what I wanted to tell you. I know the plan was to kill her but I may have an even better way. One that can give us even more money if the plan goes through."

"How much more?"

"About one hundred thousand dollars."

Suddenly she had his undivided attention. With wide eyes, he asked, "So what's the plan?"

Banker told him everything Alice wanted done, down to the last detail. When she was finished, something miraculous occurred. He was inspired to ease between her legs, to lick her clean. As her eyes rolled to the back of her head, she thought about Nine, and the feel of her breasts.

CHAPTER SIX

"No grace? No womanhood? Ah, beastly creature!"
- William Shakespeare

Gates sat at a private table in the corner of an elegant, dark restaurant, beneath the beams of the soft lights against the wall. A half-eaten prime steak sat before him on a beautiful cream-colored plate with gold accents surrounding the perimeter. Blood poured slowly out of the center of the meat and spilled onto the plate.

Preparing to finish his meal, he was bewildered when the most notorious Prophet of them all pulled a chair from a neighboring table and perched in front of him as if she'd been invited.

Stabbing a piece of juicy meat with his fork, he aimed it in her direction and asked, "Steak?"

"I'm a vegetarian," she said crossing her legs. "Don't believe in harming animals." Although in her mind, that didn't include her aunt's pesky cats.

He chuckled softly. Having limited knowledge of Nine and Alice's plight against each other, he couldn't imagine her not harming anything in her way. "And still I learn something new every day." He placed the meat into his mouth. With a gullet of food on the center of his tongue, he asked, "Tell me, Alice Prophet, what can I do you for?"

"It's not what you can do for me but what I can do for you."

He laughed. "I must tell you, I'm not a man who enjoys to be teased. Forgive me if I'm being brash. I guess you can chalk it up to old age. Whatever my rationalization, I don't have a lot of time. So what the fuck do you want?"

"Wow...I was hoping that you could at least invite a girl to your home. And give her the option of a good fuck, like I'm sure you would my cousin if I were her instead of me."

Gates sat his fork down, leaned back in the chair and looked her over. The powder blue dress with the bow underneath her neck made her appear sweet even though he knew she was as far from innocent as the seat of hell. He grabbed the white cloth napkin off the table and wiped his mouth. "Okay...I'll play. Let's go."

****

Gates tossed a log into the fireplace and took a second to be calmed by the flames and soft crackle before facing Alice. When he was awakening from his soft trance, in a Shakespearean tone, he said, *"O keep me from the worse than killing lust."*

Alice, flummoxed by his statement, tilted her head and said, "Excuse me?"

"It's Shakespeare," he said turning around, placing the fireplace poker against the side of the wall. "My apologies, Nine spoiled me. I assumed all Prophets were well-read."

"I'm sorry to disappoint you but you thought wrong," she admitted. "I'll leave Nine to the world of tales and folklore that seems to consume so much of her mind space. I much prefer to focus on what's in front of me. The here and the now."

He laughed and sat in the recliner across from her. Folding his legs, he examined her slightly scarred face and said, "Looks like someone punished you. May I ask what for?"

She rubbed her hand over the wounds. "I wouldn't say they punished me. Rather they were a little too aggressive over a disagreement. But it's okay. All's well that ends my way."

Gates nodded. "So now that we are here, be clearer, Alice Prophet. What do you want from me?"

"What I desire won't cost you a thing."

"And still I don't believe you."

She giggled. "My cousin Nine is really beautiful isn't she? Even with her blackened skin."

Gates smiled and shook his head. "What makes you think that her dark skin makes her less attractive?"

"Doesn't it?" She smirked. "Grandfather used to bleach his skin so it must be true."

"What happened to you? What turmoil do you live with every day that has caused you to see people of your own race so poorly?"

Alice grew slightly uncomfortable at Gates' successful attempt to penetrate the first layer of her internal pain. She was taught to hate herself and expressed herself in her views of other people. "You're blinded by Nine."

"And your point?"

"My point is that you'll never have her moving at the rate that you are. If you truly want my cousin, I can give her to you. And all you have to do is listen and do exactly as I say."

Gates knew she would be interesting, as all Prophets were, but her arrogance about being able to give him anything he couldn't afford was farcical. "What makes you think that I want Nine Prophet?"

"The look in your eyes every time I say her name is enough reason." Alice laughed. "So let's stop the distractions and get on with the truth. You want Nine and I can help you."

Silence.

He uncrossed his legs and poured two glasses of wine from his bar in the corner of the room. "Say that I want Nine. And say that you are in a position to give her to me, what would I have to do? And what do you want from me in return?" He handed her a glass and kept the other for himself.

"I don't want much." She crossed her legs. "Not right now anyway." She winked. "And I don't proclaim to be a matchmaker. But I do know that if you're interested in a woman like Nine Prophet you must first break down her confidence if you want to possess her. Make her self-conscious about her beauty and most of all her intelligence. You do that and in a month's time, she will belong to you." She sipped her wine.

Gates grinned. "You seem very educated on what it takes to destroy your blood relative. What makes you such a Nine expert?"

"I want to tell you but first I need you to keep an open mind."

"You can't get more open than this. So let's talk."

CHAPTER SEVEN

"So full of artless jealousy is guilt."
- William Shakespeare

Julius squirmed and screamed at the top of his lungs in an effort to be released from Nine's embrace. She did all she could to appease him and nothing seemed to work. No matter what she did, no matter what she tried, he made it known that he did not prefer her succor.

"What is it that you want from me?" she asked looking into his beautiful but horror-filled eyes. Every time he would not allow her to care for him, it broke her heart a bit more. "I am doing all I can to love you. Doing all I can to make amends for what I have done to your mother but what more can I do?"

Julius continued to cry and his wails reached another level, as if he understood every word she uttered and didn't believe her.

"I did not know my sister," she whispered as a tear fell from her eye and onto his chin. "I did not get a chance to know her but I am trying so desperately to know you. I am trying so hard to love you. Please, my sweet Julius…please allow me."

"Let me try," Chipo said stepping into the room without an invitation.

For a second, Nine wondered how much she heard about the murder of her sister and how long she'd been there. Her red and gold head wrap matched her dress with beautiful African designs. Chipo relieved Nine of the infant and the moment he was in her arms, she sang an old African nursery rhyme, called Baba Jacob, that seemed to put him in a reverie. "Baba Jacob, Baba Jacob, Usalela, Usalela…"

As she continued to sing the song, Julius grew quieter before closing his eyes and falling to sleep in Chipo's arms. When he was peaceful, she placed him down inside of the soft crib and sat on the edge of Nine's bed. She patted the spot next to her twice and Nine walked over to her and took a seat.

"Why does it seem that some women have been given the gift of motherhood while others have not?" Nine questioned, looking into Chipo's eyes. She was aware that her relationship with the old woman began with the death of her grandfather. But Chipo seemed so wise and Nine found herself drawn to her presence.

"What are your intentions?" Chipo asked softly. "With the child?"

"I care for him. Very much. I have bought him expensive clothing and am even trying hard to put him in a prestigious baby academy so that he can have a chance at a real life."

"But what are your intentions for his soul?"

Nine stood up and walked across the room. She looked out of the window at the vineyard and sighed. "I told you already. Are you so old that you can no longer hear me?" she snapped.

Although Nine was being rude, Chipo didn't take it personally because the trait she exhibited was uncharacteristic of what she'd seen since she'd been staying in Nine's home. "Money is not everything."

"You tell that to someone who has nothing, one who has lived in darkness all of her life." She crossed her arms over her chest. "I am certain she will see things differently."

"It's hard to believe but it is true. When a child enters the world, he or she is the closest a human can be to pure Source Energy...or God. And because of it, they can feel, using their emotions, when another human's intentions are off."

Nine looked over at her.

"Now when this child grows older he or she may lose the direct access to the Source because, like most older humans, their minds will be focused on things, toys, and other people's perceptions of them. It becomes harder to connect to who they really are, what they really want out of life. It becomes harder to look at themselves and say, 'I am not money, I am not this body. I am spirit.'"

"I do not say this much, Chipo, but I have to be honest. I am confused."

Chipo got up and walked slowly toward her.

"Before you begin again, I apologize for speaking to you disrespectfully a few moments ago," Nine sighed. "My words did not come from the heart."

"I never charge a person with insults from the ego." She paused. "Besides, you remind me so much of Thandi. So much of her strength is present in you. So much of her appearance that sometimes it's hard to watch you as you move around this house. It's like I'm seeing a ghost. And yet that similarity, that association, is the reason I agreed to stay for a few weeks before going back to Africa. I feel like by being around you, I am being given a chance to stop Thandi from turning into what she was before she died. The woman Kerrick made her. A woman confused of her power and her own mentality."

Nine walked away and sat on the daybed next to the window. "I am not your daughter, Chipo."

"And yet both of you had the benefit of Kerrick's rearing anyway. Of his beliefs and rigid behaviors." She paused. "Don't let him control you from the grave. Don't let him make you evil until you can't feel for others anymore." She touched her face softly. "I too remember being in the thralls of a man. I was so empty and yet filled so much by him, that I allowed him to convince me to sell Kerrick my daughter."

"What was the price?"

"Two goats," she said shamefully. "We were farmers."

Nine smiled, knowing that two goats to a farmer were equivalent to thousands of dollars.

"I was so consumed by my husband, who died some years back, that I allowed him to convince me to order vaginoplasty for Thandi to tighten up her vagina. I wanted her to remain pleasurable to Kerrick, to secure a long marriage and make him proud." She sighed. "Now look...she's gone." She gazed into Nine's eyes as if she were speaking to her own daughter again. "I put so much time into matters of outside influences that I cared nothing for her mind." She paused. "To look at you swells my heart but when you look at me, what do you feel?"

"Loved."

Chipo smiled. "The things we accrue in life are great, Nine. They allow us to forge opportunities for others and ourselves if we desire. But never allow things, money and fortunes to be a substitute for what we are put here on earth to do." She paused. "I don't know the dynamics of the Prophet family. And I must admit, I try to stay away for fear I might be stained spiritually by the knowledge of this family's customs and beliefs. But I will say this. You must love that little boy. You must love him first and in turn, he will love you back. You can't buy your place within the heart. Love him, Nine. It's the only way."

At that moment, Nine willed herself that she would try her hardest to change. Besides, what's the worst that could happen?

****

The Prophet Dinner

Victory placed a beautiful silver gravy bowl down and skipped toward the head of the table before taking a seat. Her husband Blake on the opposite end looked upon her proudly.

There was one problem with the event, white cat hair was over everything. On the plates. On the table and even the chocolate cake.

Nine and Leaf were disgusted while the others acted as if it were not there. Maybe they were used to it but Nine was not and decided not to have a thing. She wasn't there for food anyway.

Still, for the first time in almost a year, everyone was together under the guise of a wedding ceremony. They were Victory, Blake, their daughters Bethany, Samantha, and Isabel, and their only son Noel. Of course Nine and Leaf were also present. Even Marina, although half-high and frail, made an appearance with her daughter Alice, who was peering over at Nine with daggers for eyes. The only Prophet not present was Justin, Leaf's father. Then again, no one expected him to attend.

"Everyone join hands so that we can pray," Victory said, as she smiled at her kin as if they were the epitome of the perfect American family. She was doing her best to appear perfect in Nine's eyes, hoping more money would flow.

After everyone fused their hands to the closest member next to them, Victory bowed her head and began. "Lord, thank you for bringing my family together again on this blessed occasion. I thank you, Father, for bringing Nine here especially because I know she is busy and not always able to attend family functions."

Nine squeezed Leaf's hand to relieve some of the embarrassment and irritation she felt in the moment.

"I know we don't spend as much time praising you as we should, but I pray that this dinner, and the upcoming marriage of my two children will change that in your eyes," she continued. "I hope you see that we may not be like other families but at the end of the day, we try to live your—"

"You've got to be fucking kidding me," Leaf said as he released Nine and Samantha's palms. "Please tell me all of this is a joke."

"Excuse me?" Blake said as he glared his way. "My wife was praying!"

The chain of hands broke and everyone gave Leaf their undivided attention since he worked so hard for it. Nine sighed, leaned over and whispered, "What are you doing, baby? You know I am here for—"

"I can't sit here and play this fucking game," he said as he pushed back in the chair, stood up and paced the floor next to the table. "This was a mistake for me to come here."

"Come on, man," Noel said. "We just saying grace. It's not even that deep."

"You don't understand. I don't feel comfortable with any of this shit. It's one thing to do what you do, with incest and all, but now you bringing God into the picture."

"So you're extra religious now?" Samantha sighed waving at the air.

"It ain't about religion. It's about…this…all of this."

"So because we have our traditions, we don't deserve to be loved by God?" Blake questioned. "Is that what you're saying, nephew? Because it sounds like you're just like my brother, your father, always judging."

Leaf placed his hand on his forehead and looked down at the floor. He took a deep breath and gazed up at his family again. They may have appeared attractive and normal but in his perspective, they were anything but. "I'm sorry but this ain't my thing and you're not my people. My father never brought me around so I don't understand why you do the things that you do and are okay with it. I'm not like ya'll and I'll never be." He walked over to Nine and kissed her on the cheek. He could feel that she was tense and irritated but his decision to bounce was solid and he made his move for the door. "Take your time, bae. I'll be in the car making a few phone calls."

I bet you will, Nine thought.

He disappeared out of the house.

"I am sorry, ladies, but he is all mine," Nine joked as she cleared her throat. She was beyond embarrassed by his performance. Getting serious, she said, "I am sorry…he just…it is hard for him to—"

"What I find jokey is how he can condemn us and yet he is off making a family with you," Alice said slyly. "Tell me something, Nine. When he fucks you, does he call you cousin?"

"Excuse me?" Nine yelled.

"We all know he's a hypocrite, Nine. Don't act so surprised. His behavior is like the white man who sleeps with his slaves and then claims he hates niggers. You can't play both sides. At the end of the day, you must choose," Alice stated.

"You would know something about the slave mentality, since you are stuck on light skin and dark skin politics and all."

Isabel laughed but stopped when Alice gave her an evil glare.

"Nine's right and what you need to do is shut the fuck up, Alice," Marina yelled. "I'm tired of you bothering Nine and making her feel bad just because daddy left her the money instead of you." Marina looked over at Nine with pleading eyes, in an effort to ask for forgiveness. Her sunken face gave off a zombie vibe more than anything else. "Please forgive my daughter, Nine." She placed a thin hand over her heart. "I don't know what happened between you two that would cause you to cut her out of the family fortune but I support you one hundred percent."

"Mama—"

She jerked her head in her direction. "Mama, nothing," Marina yelled cutting Alice off. "Even when you were five years old, you were nothing more than a conniving bitch. Don't know why I would expect you to change when you don't have it in you. That's why the only person you could ever befriend in this family was Isabel. Everybody else too smart to hang around you."

"Excuse me?" Isabel responded, totally coherent.

"Please tell me why you felt the need to bring my child's name into the picture?" Blake asked releasing his tie to allow more air into his lungs. In case he had to blow her ass down. "Alice's inability to handle life has nothing to do with me or my children."

Alice ran out of the dining room and Isabel followed.

"Now look what you did," he said looking at Marina. "You've upset them both."

"Please save the holier than thou attitude, brother," Marina yelled. "At least I only have one kid who's fucked up as opposed to four!"

Everyone gasped.

Suddenly the affair erupted into a forum, which they used to express their bitter feelings. They yelled about whom Kerrick loved more and whom their mother favored and in the end, the entire event turned out to be a complete spectacle.

Nine allowed them to speak amongst themselves until she took too much of their resentment into her heart and gave herself a headache. "Settle down," Nine said beneath the roaring, in a quiet whisper.

But everyone was too consumed in ego, hate and bravado to consider her soft voice. This was not why she came and had she known, she would've refused her aunt's invitation and found another way to address her concerns.

She stood up and without raising her voice, every Prophet present grew silent. "I am ashamed of every one of you." She looked at all of them. "They call us freaks, in-breeders and ungodly and yet you continue to prove them right."

Marina stood up and said, "Nine, I wasn't—"

"Please do not say anything," she responded cutting her off. "I cannot take any more on. These problems are a product of grandfather's sins, not mine." She looked upon them again. "I am here because I am in the thralls of something that is very important to me. Something that, if done correctly, could set up this family for seven generations. It is a venture that is close to my heart, a wine that I am having made called *Francesca*."

"Francesca?" Victory blurted out. "After daddy's maid?"

On cue, Nine tossed a steak knife toward her aunt and it would've sliced her face if she hadn't slumped down, allowing it to stab into the wall instead. In awe, everyone looked at the trembling blade.

"That maid that you speak of took care of me. She loved me. She nurtured me and made me the woman I am today. And I will not tolerate you or anybody else speaking badly about her in this family." She lowered her head and slammed a firm fist on the table. "Understood?"

Everyone, including Victory, nodded in agreement.

"I have one request and it is that all of you stay out of the spotlight. That you refrain from getting into trouble or bringing any attention to yourselves during this process. For honoring my request, I will increase everyone's monthly allotments by five percent. Go against what I am asking and I will cut you off completely…maybe for life." She stood up, walked over to Victory and lowered her head before kissing her softly on the cheek. "Goodbye, Auntie. I am sure dinner was great."

****

Isabel's Room

Alice sat in the corner crying as Isabel did all she could to keep her own sanity and prevent from sinking into the other world with colors and amazing flashes of violence. She had her own problems but Alice was an attention hog.

"I hate my life," Alice screamed as her eyes protruded. "Nobody loves me! Nobody cares about me or what I'm going through! It's as if I'm invisible in this family! As if I'd never been born."

Isabel rubbed Alice's arm and tried to console her. "You want to do the oochie coochie? I'll go down on you this time and lick you until you say stop. I don't care how long it will take."

"No!" Alice yelled pushing her off. "I want to understand what is so bad about me that people don't like me? All I want to do is keep this family together and no one seems to care! What about me!" she yelled stabbing a fist into her palm.

Isabel positioned her body so that her head was in the center of Alice's lap, and her back was on the floor, with her knees pointed to the ceiling. She looked up at Alice and said, "Yeah...your mother was acting like a mean bitch! She's so pressed for money that she doesn't care that she's hurting your feelings. I know why you're upset. Don't worry, Alice, things will be okay."

"Mother?" Alice said coldly. "She didn't do nothing to me."

Confused on which dinner party Alice attended, Isabel said, "She was the one who embarrassed you at the party." She frowned. "Don't you remember?"

Alice shrugged and waved the air. "Oh...uh...yeah...she said a few words but it was Nine who was the meanest in the party. I saw her cruel eyes and the way she looked at me with disapproval. Like she's better than me. Mother would not have said any of those evil things if Nine didn't encourage her."

Isabel rose up and scooted away from her cousin as she tried desperately to determine who was *really* crazy.

She or Alice?

"Alice, Nine didn't say anything bad. As a matter of fact, if I'm being honest, I think I saw a hint of pity for you in her eyes. It was as if she finally understood who you are."

Isabel tried to diffuse the situation by stating the facts but all Alice could think about was Nine witnessing how much Marina hated her own child.

Humiliated, she leaped up and said, "I don't think I want to be friends with you anymore, Isabel. Mother is right, you're crazy and it may be rubbing off on me."

Isabel trembled and a tear rolled down her face. Alice might have been monstrous but she was consistent in her life and kept her company when others didn't. Bethany and Samantha were too consumed with Noel to give her any real attention. And her mother and father were only concerned about putting up fake Prophet fronts so that Nine would give them money any time they asked.

Losing Alice was not an option. "Please don't go. I'm sorry." She paused. "I won't say another word about Nine. I promise."

"Too late, crazy Izzy. You should've chosen me from the start." She clasped her hands behind her back. "I'm going to stay in one of the other rooms in the house. If you come for me, or say a word to me, I will have you killed." She walked toward the door. Before exiting, with her back faced Isabel, she said, "And don't believe for an instant that I do not possess that kind of power. If I can't hire someone, I'll simply do it myself." She walked out of the room, humming the entire way.

CHAPTER EIGHT

"As I confess, it is my nature's plague to spy into abuses and
oft my jealousy."
- William Shakespeare

W hen Alice entered her Aunt Victory's house, she
was confused to see Victory standing in the middle
of the foyer wearing black, cat hair covered underwear and
no bra. Her fleshy titties were in full swing and she was
talking to herself. She was pacing in large circles and when
she saw Alice she rushed over to her and pulled her into her
sweaty body.

When Alice wiggled away from her, Victory gripped both
sides of her arms and said, "She said no, Alice. She said no
about the money for the car as if I didn't matter!" she
screamed. "Now I'm not going to be able to afford a
wedding gift for the kids. It's embarrassing."

"You don't have any money? Or anywhere else to get
cash?" Alice asked trying to keep face and provide another
fake solution outside of her favorite.

War on Nine Prophet.

Victory looked guilty and sat on the sofa. "You don't
understand money. It's tough holding onto it if you have
responsibilities."

"You had millions though."

"When you grow up like we did, a million is a few
hundred." She paused. "When my father was alive he
would've never let me go without! And now look! I can't
even provide a wedding gift to my own kids! What kind of
mother am I? Every bride deserves a Mercedes!"

Alice tried to prevent from smiling but hearing that her
aunt was distraught by something the prized Nine did,
caused her great pleasure. The other night, at the dinner,
wore on Alice. She didn't realize how much pain she was in
until her mother embarrassed her. Not necessarily in front of
her family, but in front of Nine. Showcasing her vulnerability
inspired her even more to get revenge on Nine. She exposed

By T. Styles 79

her weak side and now it was time to show the tenacious side.

Besides, things were looking up for her. Finally her family was coming around to seeing things her way, starting with Victory. Nine had to be relieved of her power by any means accessible.

"So what does that mean, Aunt Victory? For us? For the family?"

Victory wiped the tears from her face, and flopped back on the sofa. "Oh, Alice…you're such a silly child." She crossed and uncrossed her legs. "Why must everything require action?"

"Because inaction could lead to not being prepared. Every action makes us tough and vigilant." Alice looked over at her aunt and trekked toward her. When she saw how frantic she was, she sighed. "Auntie, you act as if you don't know your true birthright at the Prophet table. Has grandfather been gone that long that you have gone blind?"

"I do know my place but—"

"But what? You continue to let that baboon run the family fortune anyway." She threw her hands up in the air. "How do we know at this point that there is even money still available? You heard her at the dinner. She entering into a new wine venture and that means putting up more capital. She's floundering everything! We'll be lucky if we'll see pennies."

Victory's voice was shaky. "We don't know how much is left."

"Exactly. I'm not asking you to do any work, Aunt Victory, except talk to the rest of the family and tell them that we have to meet. They don't trust me because they think that I'm angry over grandfather's dismissal of me in his will. And because Nine cut off only me."

"Are you bitter?"

Alice sighed and sat next to her. "I was at first. Now I understand that grandfather wasn't well before he died. He probably wasn't in his right frame of mind and she may have even poisoned him."

"Come on, Alice!" she laughed. "These productions you put on in your head should be written down." She scratched her right titty. "Even Spielberg couldn't create them."

"I'm serious!" Her eyes bulged. "How did he go from keeping her in the basement to giving her everything?"

Victory rubbed her throbbing temples, not wanting to fight a woman with such a violent passion. "You're right. I didn't even know she was alive before he introduced her at the dinner that day."

Alice focused on her aunt's lack of clothing. "Aunt Victory, why are you naked?"

"I was working out. Running around the house and stuff. I'm trying to get slim for the wedding."

Alice looked upon her and said, "You have a long way to go, don't you?"

"You have to start somewhere," Victory stated.

"Blades of orange are on fire," Isabel yelled from inside of her room. Her voice was so loud she reached octaves Alice didn't think were possible. "Blades are on fire and they're piercing our skin! Make them stop!"

Frustrated with her daughter's insane rants, Victory hopped up and rushed to see what she wanted. "I'm not sure how much I'm going to be able to deal with from Isabel. It may be time for her to go in the mental house with the other crazies where she belongs."

"We're the Prophets, Auntie. Isn't she already in the crazy house?" Alice asked.

****

Alice strolled down the street toward her car with not a care in the world when Nine pulled up in her gold Maybach. Slowly the back window rolled down and Nine peered out and ordered, "Get in."

With a noisy exhalation and a roll of her eyes, Alice said, "I was going to my car."

"It was a statement not a question." Nine leaned back in her seat and rolled the window up as she impatiently waited.

Alice looked up the street and sighed. The last thing she wanted was to be anywhere near Nine but she reasoned that with her plans in motion, everything would be going her way in time. So what were a few minutes when soon she would have millions?

So she got inside.

Once seated, she asked, "What do you want?"

"How was your day?" She was calm.

Alice frowned and attempted to hide her disdain for her boss cousin. She did an awful job and with another roll of the eyes, she asked, "Fine. Why?"

"Did you thank me for rising up this morning?" Nine asked in a soothing tone. "And having access to your day."

She gave her an incredulous stare. Confused, she said, "No."

"Well you should have, because today was the day I instructed one of my soldiers to kill you."

The strength Alice possessed moments earlier suddenly diminished.

"But I am not going to do it now, Alice. Do you know why?"

Trembling at the realization that she was supposed to be taken from this earth, she said, "No."

"Because I am going to give you a chance to hang yourself. I am going to give you a chance to stay out of my way. Maybe, just maybe, we will have a relationship in the future."

With bulging eyes, she asked, "Why would you do that?"

Nine sighed. "Because I saw the look on your face when your mother spoke to you so harshly at dinner. And I know what it feels like not to have the love of your birth mother. Before you and I, Prophet women in this family were weak." She paused. "I am not condoning what you did to me; you were the cause of some of my worst nightmares. But suddenly things make sense and I want to give you a chance to do what is right." Nine touched her leg. "Do not make me kill you, Alice. Do not make me regret this day because if I do, your passing will not be unchallenging. There will be nothing but dark days ahead for you if you fuck up. And you will beg me for the day that your soul will be released and it will never come." She looked into her eyes. "Do you hear me? Never come."

Alice readjusted in her seat, while two drops of sweat rolled down her forehead and fell into her eyes.

"I am offering a chance that I never thought was possible for you. For us." Nine swallowed. "To start all over." She raised her hand for Alice to shake it. "Do you want this gift?"

Alice looked down at Nine's well-manicured fingers and slowly shook her hand. "Yes, I do…thank…thank you," she whispered.

When Alice got out of Nine's car, she waited until it was out of sight. When she was gone she rushed to the side of Victory's house and threw up in the rose bushes.

Her insides didn't stop rocking until she saw blood.

CHAPTER NINE

"Fear not thy sons; they shall do well enough."
- *William Shakespeare*

Nine sat on a plush baby blue sofa clutching Leaf's hand. Julius was wrapped up in a blanket, lying in her lap, and when she looked down at him, she grinned when she saw that he was peaceful. Although it was Banker who put him to sleep, she was able to enjoy him in the moment.

To her left was Banker and as always, she held a pencil and paper in her hand, eager to receive orders.

While Nine waited on the director of Royal Babies to meet with them and explain the curriculum, she glanced at the huge picture of a beautiful black baby on the wall in front of her. A gold frame surrounded it, making the child appear larger than life. She envisioned herself as a baby although no pictures of her existed. She resolved to commission a painting of Julius as soon as possible.

Feeling nervous, Nine snaked her fingertip into the palm of Leaf's hand. When he looked down at his wife's slender hand, he eased his arm around the back of her chair before pulling her toward the side of his body. "This is a new look on you," he said kissing the top of her forehead.

"What is that?"

"Nervousness."

She shook her head and looked down at Julius. "I just want the best for him, Leaf. I want him to have the kind of lifestyle that—"

"We would've given our son if he would've remained alive," he said finishing her sentence.

She nodded yes.

Leaf kissed her lips. "Bae, whether he gets into this bourgeoisie ass school or not, with you in his life he's already destined." He ran his hand alongside her face. "Because you love him despite his mother and what she did to us by killing our child."

He lowered his voice when he saw Banker staring directly at the pinkness of his tongue. Most people who were eavesdropping would have at least tried to hide it. Unfortunately, Banker had no cut cards and got caught.

"You good, shawty?" he asked Banker. "'Cause you staring hard."

Embarrassed, she closed her mouth, ran her tongue around it because it dried out due to being opened, and said, "Sorry."

"I don't like that girl," he whispered. "Something's off with her."

"You are just repelled by her because she works for me."

"It's amazing. You can be one of the most intelligent or dumbest people in the world if you try hard enough," he said shaking his head. "Please don't tell me you actually believe that shit."

Seconds later, a tall slender black woman with a pointed nose waltzed over to them. She was dressed in a designer suit, which made her appear stuffy as opposed to fashionable and approachable. In her early thirties, the lines on her forehead already penetrated her skin, causing her to age ten more years.

Banker stood up and shook the woman's hand. "Hello, Vanique," she smiled. "These are my bosses I was telling you about over the phone." Banker looked at the baby. "And that is Julius...he's sleeping."

Nine and Leaf rose and with a fake smile plastered on Vanique's face, she outstretched her fingertips. First, she jiggled Nine's hand before moving to Leaf's. She didn't bother to look at the baby. This was about business not cuteness.

"It's great to meet you. Banker has told me so much about you. Prior to this day, I thought Julius belonged to her. It's great to see his real parents." Her grip was cold and she released quickly. "Now if I can get your real name, I'll be good."

"Excuse me?" Nine hesitated.

"She gave me your nickname earlier and I felt uncomfortable at first approving your application. Especially after it was denied before—"

"Before you found out we owned Aristocrat Hills," Leaf said interrupting her. He didn't fuck with the bitch. "It's amazing how a little money can change an opinion around here."

She smiled and tried to conceal her guilt. "You caught me," she replied with raised hands, colorless palms facing their direction. "We are guilty of wanting the children of Royal Babies to be around the elite of our society." She dropped her hands at her sides. "And based on your stature, with owning Aristocrat Hills and all, I'm sure young Julius will fit right in." She smiled and looked into Nine's eyes. "But first, what is your real name?"

"Marie Antoinette," Nine blurted out, losing the cool she once possessed. "Lincoln." She swallowed. "Marie Antoinette Lincoln."

Both Leaf and Banker gazed at her oddly.

They could look at her crazy all they wanted. But she had no intentions on telling Vanique that she was a Prophet, only for her to forge opinions about their in-breeding practices that were created before she was born.

"Ah," Vanique smiled brightly. "With a name like that, young Julius Lincoln will be a star here. Wow…Julius Lincoln, it just rolls off the tongue." She slapped her hands together and rubbed them briskly. "Before we go and sign the paperwork, I hope you and your husband will join us tonight for the benefit gala. All contributions will go to BBIN, Black Babies In Need Foundation." She looked between them. "Can we count on your contribution…I mean…participation tonight?"

****

Leaf sat in the backseat and looked over at his wife with abhorrence. After what she pulled in the daycare center, he was starting not to recognize her anymore. "Why would you lie in there, Nine? Why you putting on a show for a bunch of uppity niggas? All she has to do is look at the news and see our faces plastered everywhere from that wine conference you made me go to."

"How am I putting on a show, Leaf?" she responded coolly. "You are just afraid to fit into society even if it will help Julius."

"How the fuck you sound? Huh? First off, we make enough money so that neither one of us has to work again in this lifetime. Or Julius, his kids, their kids and his side bitches! You don't even have to run the drug operation if you don't want to, because you know the Nobles can do it. So don't tell me that by kissing some black bitch's ass, I'll be helping my son." He paused. "What I really want to know right here and right now is why did you lie?"

"About what?" She moved around uneasily and was too proud to admit her wrong.

"Everything, Nine! But let's start with your name!"

"I am not my name, Leaf. What does it matter what they choose to call me?" She looked in the backseat at Julius who was still sleeping peacefully. "Just as long as he has the best lifestyle befitting a king."

He looked at her with lowered brows, disappointed in her conduct. "I'm sick of you and them fucking fairytale books! That shit you be reading is not real, Nine! You can't be fitting of this or fitting of that! And if you ever ran out of money, you would see that all of the shit you doing don't matter! Because not one of your men would stand by you if you can't drop that paper. If you can't afford to pay them. All that matters is Julius and me. Not some fake ass bitch in a daycare center."

Nine's heart rate increased but she was trying desperately to retain her cool demeanor. Besides, it was unladylike to be rude. "Do you know that Royal Babies teaches children to play Bach at the age of four? And Mozart at six?"

"And none of that shit will matter in the real world! Let's see how Mozart and Bach help the little nigga if he gets a burner placed to the back of his head."

"Now who is thinking about him in a deadly way?"

"I'm serious! When I asked you to be my wife, do you know what you said to me?"

"He will be fluent in five languages before he is even in high—"

"Do you remember what you said?" he yelled.

Nine looked away and outside of the window to her left. "That I would love you forever but out of respect, I could never take another name other than Prophet."

"That shit hurt, Nine. You even said it recently. But I dealt with it because it wouldn't change how I felt about you." He paused. "And now you use my last name for an overrated daycare center when it suits you? What type shit is that?" He paused. "Do you even know who Marie Antoinette was?"

"Oh, Leaf, do not be ridiculous."

"Tell me!"

She laughed. "Do not be disrespectful, Leaf. You just accused me of believing in fairytales. Of course I know who she was. Besides being the Queen of France, she was also—"

"Called L'Autrichienne," he said with a learned French accent. Although Nine was versed on the customs of the eighteenth century, her husband knew four languages, one of them being French.

Nine gazed over at him, not sure whether to be turned on or disrespected by his attempt to make her look foolish. "L'Autrichienne is French for the word whore...bitch. Did you know that after awhile, Marie was hated by her own people, Nine? And was considered to be wasteful and promiscuous. She wasn't even educated. And that's the kind of woman you want to abandon your last name to be?"

"Cousin, you are so busy trying to look down on me that you make yourself appear ignorant. Outside of her downfalls, did you know that although she was not formally trained, just like me, she was self-taught before reining in the family? With our backgrounds being so similar, I guess you should ask yourself this question, cousin. Are you sure that I am the kind of woman you want to remain married to?"

Leaf shook his head and laughed. "You put me and your assistant in a fucked up position just now. And played yourself as fake. I can only imagine what that chick is thinking about us on her way home."

"Stop being melodramatic."

"I'm not going to that bullshit ass event tonight so don't drop your jaw to ask. I'll have a few of my soldiers take twenty stacks to a few neighborhoods I know need it the most. I do that kind of thing anyway. At least then I'll know my money will get to the appropriate place." He hopped out of the car and hit the top of the hood twice. "Johnson," he said addressing the driver, "take my wife and child home." He slammed the door and walked away. "I'll get up with you when I can, Marie Antoinette. Or would you prefer whore?"

****

Nine stood behind a tall black podium with gold lining, holding a green Parakeet. She long since pushed the argument with her husband out of her mind although the spirit of the disagreement lingered in the air. It was now time for business.

Before her was a sea of men seated in an auditorium built especially for them on the outskirts of her property, at the base of Aristocrat Hills. They were almost a thousand of the most violent men ever put together and yet they were composed, each looking upon their boss with admiration and even lust.

No longer were they their pasts, mistakes or aggressions. From the moment Nine recruited them and gave them each a new name, together they were The Legion.

They were one.

"This is an Australian parakeet called the budgerigar," Nine said, each word slow, polished and powerful. "On the surface, it appears to be a gentle bird. Non-threatening and vulnerable even. Yet many a black falcon have attempted to eat this animal only to fail." She strolled from behind her podium and toward one of the aisles.

Looking down at her men, she continued. "Why is that? Why does the falcon try but often flounder?" She stroked the bird's back with her index finger. "I will tell you why," she smiled. "Because of a phenomenon called a swarm. Every day, thousands of this little guy will get with other budgerigars and fly together in a pack. When this happens, the black falcon may try and infiltrate, by flying into the swarm, but he is always unsuccessful. In the end, the organized chaos will prove to be too confusing and the black falcon will give up and find another prey. A single prey that has left his team."

She tossed the bird in the air and it flapped its wings lightly only to be eaten by a black falcon, which was waiting in the corner.

Hiding.

They may not have seen it but she knew it was there.

After watching the bird be eaten, she addressed her men again. "Working together is the only way the budgerigar survives. Working together, they will always outwit and outnumber the black falcon. But the moment one separates from the flock, it will be on its own and if it is not careful, there is no coming back."

She walked back to the podium and there wasn't a person in the building who was not pulled in by her charm.

"We must move together with a single purpose. We must be kind to our families and take care of our children. Our responsibilities. We must give back to our communities. But above all, we must take care of one another. No matter who we have to kill."

****

After the meeting, Nine walked out of The Academy, a section of property where her men were trained and practiced shooting. Antonius was walking leisurely with her and Nine's hands were clutched behind her back. "How is your daughter?"

He laughed. "Upset…but she is doing better about Mo's death. Surprisingly, she doesn't blame me for his murder."

"Oh? Who does she blame?"

"The beautiful monster," he chuckled.

"And that is?"

"You."

Nine smiled. "I do not take it personally. I am used to holding misplaced blame," she said as she thought about her family. "In some ways, it makes me stronger." She paused. "Tell me something, Antonius, are you with your daughter's mother?"

"No…not for some time now. I'll be honest and say it was my fault we weren't successful. I wasn't ready for a relationship, and she wasn't ready for the games I played while running the streets. If I have one regret in life, and I don't have many, it's letting her get away."

Nine nodded. "Do you have a girlfriend, Antonius?"

He laughed. "There's only time in my life for one woman, Nine. And that is you."

She blushed.

"Why do you ask?"

She thought about the problems she was having with Leaf. His recent judgment of her and her need to be successful in the wine venture. Instead, she left it alone, preferring to remain private. "No reason," She paused. "What do you think about the human psyche?"

Antonius looked at her before quickly looking away. Beautiful or not, it was considered rude to stare the alpha in the eyes. "Personally, I don't believe there are any limits to what we are capable of. Our refusal to have limits is the reason we are so powerful. Why do you ask?"

They stopped walking and turned to watch the men fire at the black targets on white paper. With .45 handguns in their clasps, each soldier continued to meet their marks smack dab in the center.

All except Galileo.

"It has always been a consideration of mine." She shrugged. "Curiosity eats at me sometimes and I question things like that." She focused on Galileo. "So how is he?"

"A handful. He wants me to pay him for his six month payout early," Antonius said in exhaustion. Oh how he wished she'd just fire his bum ass and get it over with. "Sounds to me like he's planning to go somewhere."

"And what are you going to do?"

"He says it's for his kid. And that he needed to pay his tuition." He paused. "But when I checked with his baby's mother, she said he hadn't given her any money or stopped by to see his son in over a year. He's fucking with some new chick who has his head wrapped up."

Nine's temples throbbed. One of the rules for her men was to take care of their families and their community. And Galileo's lax behavior about his family enraged her. "So what are you going to do?"

"I don't know. That's why I'm coming to you."

Nine exhaled and then smiled at him. She liked him a lot and respected how he handled business so she didn't want to tell him what to do. It was important to guide him to think on his own. "Men work better when they are inspired. When they have something to look forward to. It's the reason I scheduled their payments twice a year because they'll work harder knowing that if they fail to give it their best, at any moment everything they're doing will be for nothing. They could lose everything." She smiled at him. "Make a decision, Antonius, and whatever it is, I will support you."

Nine walked over to Galileo. He was holding his gun and firing repeatedly off-center of his target. She strolled behind him and wrapped her arms around his body, so that both of their hands were touching the weapon at the same time. Before speaking, she took a moment and remembered the exact words her dearest Fran said to her when she was learning to shoot.

With her lips closely against his cool earlobe, almost in a sexual manner, she whispered, "Whenever you hold a weapon, the only thing on your mind should be your target and your aim." She paused. "If your mind is on anything else, it could cost you your life. Are we clear?"

Frightened by the solo attention she was giving him, he nodded yes.

"Now fire."

He hit his target.

"Take care of your son, Galileo, before I do things to you, you could never imagine."

****

Gates and Nine were face-to-face, swaying on the dance floor. As always, five members of The Legion, including Antonius and Nine's cousin Noel, stayed in the background to ensure that no one walked within her space.

She was protected at all times.

Nine's delicate fingers rested in the palm of his hand as he gazed down into her eyes. Since Leaf was not willing to escort her to the Royal Babies function, out of spite, she invited Gates. And as always, he jumped at the honor to be in her presence. *"If it proves so, then loving goes by haps. Some Cupids kill with arrows, some with traps,"* Gates quoted.

Nine giggled, since she was quite well versed on Shakespeare. "From the play, *Much Ado About Nothing*," she said correctly.

Pleased she knew the verse, and that he was amongst worthy company, he said, "I don't trust your cousin Alice." He continued to lead her body to the melody.

Nine grinned. "I take it you have been in her presence recently."

"Yes, and she isn't a Nine Prophet fan."

She wondered did they speak before or after their last conversation. "I am not worried about my cousin. We have our date and time. She just does not know it yet."

"So let me get this right, you know she's dangerous and still you keep her around?" he asked with raised brows.

"Do you know why enemies are so sweet?"

He chuckled. "I want to laugh at your naivety and yet by being around you, I've learned that there is always a method to your dementia."

Nine giggled and pressed the side of her face against his chest. His heart rate increased and she inhaled deeply. "When you know who your enemies are, and you play them well, they keep you on your toes. You can close your eyes, and even if they have a gun aimed in your direction, you can still prevent being shot." She looked up into his eyes. "Enemies are nothing more than coaches keeping you sharp. It is the ones whom you do not know about who are savage."

He wiped the hair out of her face and tucked it behind her ear. "I want you to be safe, Nine."

"Why?"

"So that eventually you'll come to me, where you belong."

She giggled. "You know that will never happen, Sir Gates. Leaf and I are at odds but he is still my husband. He was the first man who ever looked upon me at my lowest and lifted me up. Where I was. Without all of the bells and whistles I have now. I will always remember him for that and my loyalty will never waiver. Ever."

"And yet when I look into your eyes, I can tell that if it were not for him, it would be the two of us." He paused. "You favor older men, Nine. Most powerful women do."

Nine separated from him and walked toward the table. He followed, as if possessed, pulling her chair out before she sat down. She took a seat, crossed her legs and waited for him to sit across from her. "Where do we stand with Baltimore, Sir Gates?" she grinned. "Have you given any more consideration to using my product only? Or perhaps stepping down for retirement?"

"You bring me here to discuss business?"

"What better time than amongst music and wine?" She raised her glass.

He nodded and tried to conceal his irritation. "We do need better quality cocaine. But from what I'm told, your connect is in a bind and unable to deliver. Even if I wanted to use him, he is at war with the Russians and that adds a complication to my business that I'm not willing to bear."

"Trust me when I say that the Russians will not be a concern for long. You and your associates are an important part of my organization. I wish you would allow us to join forces. All I want to do is ensure that we all increase our profit margins. I want what is in your best interest, Sir Gates. At times, I can be possessive. I do not want anybody else selling you coke. In a sense, it is almost as if you belong to me."

"The way you talk to me, sometimes I feel as if I do." He paused. "Please, let's just enjoy ourselves and have our trustees deal with those issues later." He paused. "Besides, the night is still young and tomorrow you'll have to answer to Leaf for our evening. When that happens, who knows when I'll be able to see you again." He raised his glass. "To the present."

She raised hers and clinked it gently against his. "To the future."

When she took a sip, suddenly a beautiful girl with dark eyes and long hair entered the event. She was dressed in an inexpensive long black gown. When she and Nine made eye contact, she smiled at Nine in a manner Nine couldn't decipher

Finally, she walked away.

Who was she? Nine thought.

CHAPTER TEN

"Wisely and slow; they stumble that run fast."
- *William Shakespeare*

The mid-afternoon glow from the open windows spilled into the Prophet mansion, as Nine sat in the living room, sipping a glass of red wine. It was her favorite. She was thinking about her evening with Gates and how Leaf would react when he was fully awake. Although she didn't tell him on the onset that she was inviting Gates, he knew the limits she'd reach to attain revenge. He was aware she would invite him before she did.

Spite was her favorite game.

Upon readjusting in her seat, she was suddenly keyed in to the sound of the workers building inside of the mansion. It was like music to her ears because soon the final additions she was placing on her home would be complete, and like a child on Christmas Eve, she anticipated the day.

When she gazed toward her right, Julius lay asleep peacefully in the basinet a few feet over from the table. He cooed a little and she sat the glass down on the end table, picked him up and pulled him into her arms to settle his spirit.

Looking down at him, she remembered the things Chipo said to her. She would try to love him as she would her own, hoping all would be well.

"I pray that I can raise you strong. To be a man of honor and courage. Possessing all of the strong things about grandfather and the good things about Leaf."

A smile rested on her face until she saw a dark figure from the corner of her eye. Horrified, she placed the baby inside of the crib, spilling her wine in the process. Once he was down, she unlatched the 9mm handgun from under the table and advanced toward the direction of the silhouette.

The quicker she progressed, the swifter the figure ran until finally it disappeared into the room where Kerrick used to tear into her flesh with leather whips. Without cutting on the lights, she pointed into the darkness and fired four times. When the smell of gunfire wafted through her nostrils, she turned the light on. Across the way, she saw four bullet holes in the wall that she made.

But no being.

Slowly she moved toward the gunshots and ran her hand across the punctures. There was no one there but the gaps from her hot bullets were real. "Where did you go?" she said to herself spinning around. "I know I saw you in here. I cannot be losing my mind." She paused. "Can I?"

When she heard the baby crying from the monitor on her watch she ran toward him. "Julius! I'm coming! I am so sorry!"

****

Nine and Leaf stood nervously next to Dr. Banning, the same physician who birthed Nine and all the Prophet children. The doctor pressed a stethoscope against Julius' chest to hear his tiny heartbeat as Nine and Leaf hung behind until the verdict was given. When Dr. Banning was finished, she dropped her instrument around her neck and walked over to them.

"He's fine," she whispered. "You have nothing to be worried about." She smiled lightly.

Nine exhaled a sigh of relief and placed her hand over her heart. "But...what about..."

"He sucked the wine you spilled on his pajamas but it wasn't enough to hurt him. I see how much you care for him, Nine. Try not to worry. It's obvious that you love your son. So be easy with that thought because all mothers make mistakes."

Unlike Nine's normal calm disposition, she was now an emotional wreck. Pacing in place, she stopped abruptly and said, "I...almost...killed..."

"Honey," Dr. Banning said pressing her cool hands on the sides of her face. "This was not your fault and I can't allow you to take that into your heart. Give yourself a break.

You reached me in time." Suddenly the first woman who touched her as a baby placed her mind at ease.

"Thank you," Nine said. "I'll have Banker write you a check for…"

"Don't worry about that. Every month for the past thirty years, the Prophet family has sent me a check, even if I wasn't caring for them. The only thing I did was my job." She touched Leaf on the hand too. "Call me if you both need anything else." She smiled and walked out of the room.

When she left, Leaf led Nine out of the room so that the baby could sleep peacefully. Sitting at the dining room table, she looked out at the vineyard. "Leaf, am I crazy? Did I see someone or am I really losing my mind?"

Worried about his wife's mental health, he walked toward the cabinet in the kitchen and made coffee. He prepared it like she wanted and looked into her eyes. "I don't approve of what you did last night, Nine. And if you ever do something like that again, I will leave you." He turned the coffee pot on, leaned against the counter and folded his arms over his chest. "Are you in love with Gates?"

"I am asking you if I am crazy and this is what you say to me?"

"I've witnessed you be abused by your grandfather, starved and even forgotten about for weeks. You've always come out of the darkness able to see the light." He paused. "But our marriage is another matter. Are…you…in…love…with…Gates?"

"Of course not."

"Then why won't you let me kill him?"

"You know he has Baltimore in his pocket and I want it."

"You could convince his partners to side with you. And then you won't need him. There has to be another reason, a petty one, and I'm going to find out."

"Leaf, it is not that deep."

"Do you want to remain in this marriage or not?"

"Of course I do!"

"Well, never disrespect me again by being seen with another man. Am I clear?"

Nine crossed her legs. "I hear you, cousin."

When the coffee was done, he poured her a black cup and sat next to her at the table. "For humor purposes only, I'll answer your earlier question. No, I don't think that you're crazy. But what I do think you're doing is taking on too much. The wine venture, the drug operation, Chipo, who I happen to like, and this wedding. Too much is happening, Nine." He placed his hand on her thigh. "Bae, you spent all of your life beneath this house. Not inside of it. Don't do so much where you lose your sanity."

Nine gazed at him but she detached from the conversation a long time ago. She hated to be reprimanded. Suddenly she remembered his private text messaging sessions. "Leaf, there was a girl at the event last night. A pretty girl with long black hair and dark eyes. Do you know her?"

He removed his hand, guilt covering him like a coat. "Why would I unless I saw a picture?"

"Because she came into the party and just stared at me. Like she knew me."

"Did she speak to you?"

"No."

"Unless I saw her, I can't be sure who she is. Besides, I know a lot of people."

She stood up and walked in front of him. Bending down slightly, she kissed him on the lips. "I am going to take another shower. Thank you for loving me, Leaf."

He laughed at her. The statement was her way of saying, *you got your shit with you and so do I,* and all he could do was smile.

When she disappeared into the house, he removed the cell phone from his pocket and called a number. When the person he wanted to speak with answered, he got right down to business. "This is my final warning and there will not be another. Stay the fuck away from my wife."

"You're a child, Leaf," Gates responded. "Or should I call you Autumn? The birth name you were given?" He paused. "Whatever it is, what makes you think that you could handle a woman of Nine's caliber? If I don't try my hand, someone else will. Be grateful you know me. Better it be the man whose child you murdered than someone else."

Leaf tried to contain himself although he felt his breaths weighing heavily within his chest cavity. "I've warned you and I will not say it again. Nine Prophet belongs to me. Since the day I found her under this house. And if you don't respect that, there will come a time when you will beg me for mercy. And I will remember this moment."

****

Since Chipo would be leaving in a few days to return to Africa, she decided to show Nine how to prepare a classic African breakfast called Fit-Fit (a type of bread). With the Prophet family being direct decedents of Africa, by way of Kerrick, she wanted Nine to know as much about her people and culture as possible.

Leaf was out of the house and Nine remained home because ever since Julius sipped the wine, he would cry every hour, drying out his throat and making himself hoarse in the process. Dr. Banning had been to the mansion five times, each time claiming nothing was wrong. Finally, three days had passed since the accident and he was able to get some sleep.

"This was Thandi's favorite when she was a child," Chipo said as she scooped a bowl for herself and Nine. "When she got older, and cared more for her figure, she wouldn't enjoy it as much. Not around her husband anyway." She grinned as if she could see her face. "But whenever she left Kerrick for the day and came home, we'd share the meal, no matter what time of day."

Leaf was out with Noel and Banker was running errands so Nine cherished the moment alone. It was like she had her all to herself. "What was she like? Thandi." Nine asked. She took a seat. "I am fascinated by the only woman grandfather ever loved."

"Nonsense, I'm sure he loved your grandmother, honey."

"He did not." She shook her head slowly, remembering the distance Kerrick slid in between him and his wife. "I got the impression that every woman he was with was a consolation prize. Even my white grandmother."

Chipo sighed. "Well, let me see. Thandi was spicy," she giggled, "for lack of better words. But she was also as smart as a whip. A mathematician who had a deep love for astronomy. She always dreamed big and was interested in the universe. Yes...my sweet baby was born way before her time."

Nine was surprised at how much they had in common. Thandi sounded as thirsty as she was for knowledge. "Why did she not go to college? And pursue her dreams?"

Chipo's head dropped in shame. "In Africa, a woman's place is behind her man. So she gave up the desire to reach heights for fear Kerrick would find her unattractive. However, I believe she had a plan. I believe if she made it to America, he would've had his hands full trying to control her."

"Why do you say that?" she asked, glued on to every word.

"Child, I don't know much but I know this. That baby of mine would've attended every college course available in your country. Such a shame that so many black women don't take advantage of the opportunities. When people in my country don't have many." She paused. "Just the other day, Leaf showed me how to use the YoopTube."

"YoopTube?" Nine giggled. "Do you mean YouTube?"

Chipo laughed heartedly and fell back into her seat. "Yes. The YouTube. I wanted to learn how to make a meal for Leaf, since you both showed me generosity. I was in awe at the different things you could learn! Whether it be how to play an instrument or how to prepare a meal, it's all there."

Nine grinned. "You and Leaf eat dinner together?"

"Oh yes, honey, on so many nights," she laughed. "Since your maid has been on sick leave, we'd just sit at this table and talk about life."

"Where was I?"

"Handling business," Chipo said gazing into her eyes. She wanted her to remember her expression and be reminded of the importance of spending time with family. She was an old woman, but if she could get quality time with her husband, a sexier woman could too. "He's so fascinating. Not sure where you two met but Leaf loves you very much."

Nine lowered her head in shame. She would have to make it her business to treat him better or risk losing him, for this she was certain.

Suddenly Chipo's disposition changed to a serious tone. "Nine, you are in the land of opportunity. What my ancestors, and yours, wouldn't give for the chance to learn. To thrive! You can be whomever you want in here," she pointed to Nine's head, "and here," she pointed at her heart.

"Oh, Chipo, please allow me to continue to send money to you in Africa," Nine said excitedly. "It will be my pleasure to build more than one school in Thandi's name."

"You don't have to do that, child." She waved her off.

"I know. I do it because I want to."

Chipo smiled and said, "Thank you. If the gift was just for me, I would refuse, but so many young people could benefit. So thank you again."

When Nine's cell phone rang, she was angry because Chipo was like an orb of energy and whenever she was around her she wanted to suck up as much of her wisdom as possible. "Excuse me. I have to take this call. I will be right back."

"Go ahead, child. I'm here."

Nine grabbed her phone and walked toward the living room when she saw Victory's number on the screen. She figured she was about to ask about money for Bethany's Benz, which Nine secretly had intentions on giving her anyway…just closer to the wedding day instead of now.

Victory was draining. Every five minutes, she asked for money, when Nine knew full well what she gave her each month provided for her needs and then some. Where her money went, only Victory knew.

Furthermore, Kerrick left his fortune to her, without instructions on sharing. If she refused to give them a shiny cent, she would be well within her legal rights. It was Nine who decided to break bread with the family, as opposed to hoarding the cash for herself. Even though not one of them helped her in her hour of need.

"Yes, Victory." Nine looked over at Chipo and smiled as she sang the song that always put Julius to sleep. "I am busy right now, so make it quick."

"Something terrible has happened!"

Nine's eyebrows rose. "What now?" she yelled, forcing Chipo to rush toward her.

"Samantha and Bethany are in prison!"

"For what?"

"Fighting on an airplane."

Nine's heart rate kicked up even though she remained as cool as the breeze. "Because of what?"

"Because of Noel! Oh, Nine, please come over! This is a family emergency and we need your help! I don't know what to do. Bring your checkbook though because we will need an attorney."

This can't be happening right now, Nine thought. *I just had a conversation with them!*

"I am on my way!"

"But it's not the worst of it," she sighed.

"What can be worse than this, Victory? You have already single handedly ruined my day. What else could it be now?"

"I'm so sorry, Nine. But this issue has made it to the news!"

****

Nine sat in front of Harry Dance, the director of The Coliseum Winery, exhausted and anxious in the same breath. Despite all the money in her bank account, and all of the power at her disposal, at the moment, she felt like a child sitting in front of the school principal.

"Is it true?" he asked from behind his large, intimidating desk. His pointed nose sprouted unusually long hairs that flagged every time he breathed.

Upon his line of questioning, Nine moved uneasily in her seat. Antonius, who accompanied her, sat next to her for support because she was too embarrassed to tell Leaf about the ordeal.

She didn't want him knowing that her family was caught up in the news for the fight and that they were facing federal charges. But more than anything, that she dropped one hundred thousand dollars for their legal defense and was begging the winery to keep the deal in place.

"Which part are you speaking of?" Nine asked.

"Your family." He cleared his throat. "I received news that your family are in-breeders."

Nine swallowed and crossed her legs, hoping to appear honest. "No. It is not true." A small sweat bead rolled down her face and she swatted it away.

"Then why is Channel 9 reporting that your cousins," he looked around his desk and located a piece of paper. When he found it he pointed at it and said, "Bethany and Samantha Prophet, were fighting on an airplane about who their brother loves most? Causing the plane to make an emergency landing at an unscheduled location." He looked up at Nine. "Is it true?"

"I am not sure...I..."

"Sir, people make up things in the news every day," Antonius interjected. "You're a CEO and I know you know that. As a matter of fact, you were involved in a scandal with a young secretary—"

"And that was thrown out because the allegations were false!"

"Exactly," Antonius said calmly. "When you have money, people lie. It comes with the business."

He readjusted in his seat. "And you are?"

"I'm Mrs. Prophet's business partner."

The director sat back in his seat. "Oh...I see."

Antonius looked over at Nine and when she didn't appear ready to go through with the meeting, he proceeded. "Listen, don't miss out on a major business opportunity with Mrs. Prophet because you believe a deception."

The director moved uneasily in his seat. "I hope you are being truthful. I sure would hate to pull out of this deal but for the reputation of my company, I would have to." He paused. "In other words, make this problem go away or we're done."

CHAPTER ELEVEN

"Thou canst not come to me: I come to thee."
- William Shakespeare

The shades were drawn in Nine's bedroom so that she could get some rest and possibly an escape from her ratchet life. First, she discovered that her family did exactly what she forbade them to do...get caught up in the press. And when she came home after the meeting, she found a goodbye letter from Chipo, only to learn that she left without actually saying goodbye.

The date for her departure was always the same. It was just that the troubles of the world caused Nine to forget that she was leaving.

She was about to roll over and get some more sleep when the phone rang. Instead of reaching for it, she pressed the pillow over her head. "Leaf," she whispered. "Get that." When the phone rang again she said, "Baby, please get the phone."

When she threw the pillow off her head and rubbed her hand over the cool mattress, she sighed. He wasn't there. Using the little energy she possessed, she crawled to the other side of the bed and snatched the phone off the hook, squashing the handset against her ear. "Hello."

"Good morning, beautiful niece," Victory sang. She was in the wrong mood. "I was calling to see how you're doing."

Nine sighed, rolled over on her back and placed her other hand on her forehead. "Did Samantha and Bethany get home yet?"

"Not yet," she sighed. "But I know the prison will release them any day now. I'm just waiting for their bail amount from the lawyer you attained." She paused. "Thank you for helping me pay for it."

Helping? Bitch, I paid it all!

Nine tried desperately to hold her anger but she made a way. The only thing she wanted was to let the situation subside and get the Francesca venture off the ground. And if it meant keeping the peace with her family, then so be it. "Not a problem, Aunt Victory. When you get the exact amount let me know."

She was about to hang up when Victory yelled, "Wait!"

Nine rolled her eyes. "What do you want now?"

"Wow, aren't we grumpy this morning?"

"What do you need, Victory?" Nine said in a serious tone.

"I know you told me no about the car money because I keep asking but I'm really hoping you will reconsider. I still want to give Bethany a wedding gift but now there's another problem."

Nine sat up in the bed and crossed her arms over her chest. "What now?"

"It's Isabel. I don't know what's going on with her. I believe it has something to do with her and Alice not talking anymore. They got into a spiff a few days back and neither is telling me what happened. But now...well now, she's been mentally unstable. I might have to put her in a facility, Nine. Of course, I can't afford to do it. Things are not like they used to be since daddy died."

Breathing heavily through her nose, Nine said, "What is the matter with her?"

"Just a lot of snapping and talking to people who aren't there. The usual but it's just happening more."

Nine sighed. "I will be by to check on her in the morning. I will make a decision then."

"Thank you so much, niece."

"I am talking about the facility, Victory. The verdict is still out about the car, since at the very least, the wedding will be postponed until next year. That is, if they do not get convicted."

"I know and I love you so much for helping me." She paused. "I'll talk to you when you get here. Bye!"

"If I were you, I wouldn't give her another dime, bae," Leaf said walking into the room. He flipped on the light and sat on the edge of the bed. His body was glistening with sweat, which meant he had been in the gym downstairs working out. "She's using you."

"But she said it is for Isabel this time."

Leaf sighed. "The nigga Kerrick left you the money. If he wanted them to have it, he would've written it in his will."

"The nigga you are talking about happens to be our grandfather. Not just mine."

"I don't respect a man who would demand that his children breed amongst each other. Why I gotta keep telling you that when you know my stance?" He paused. "Now look at the news. Every time I turn around, I see a story about you and me. And the Prophet family." He paused. "People thinking I'm like them...with the incest and shit."

Nine rubbed her temples. "Do you love me?"

"Yes."

"Then you are with the incest shit," Nine said emphatically. "If there is one thing about grandfather's philosophy that I respect, it is that we are superior. And mixing bloodlines could taint that."

"When I fell in love with you, I didn't know," he said standing up. He walked toward the window and opened the curtains. "There was no way I was going to turn my back and walk out on you at that point. I was already gone."

Nine strolled over to him and snaked her arms around his waist. "What did you tell me when I was pregnant and had some reservations about us being cousins and in a relationship?"

He sighed. "I said that we were already in love and that our life didn't have to be like anybody else's." He paused. "But sisters and brothers...I just can't understand that." He turned around and faced her. "At the same time, I don't want this lifestyle for Julius."

"Every family is given a set of rules by which they operate. Ours is in-breeding and getting money, cousin. And that is okay. If we are all in agreement, where is the dishonor in that?"

Leaf sighed, realizing he was not getting through to her. "I don't accept it and I never will."

"Unfortunately, that is a decision you do not get to make on your own. When it comes to Julius anyway. I am hoping that at some point, I will birth a beautiful baby girl. And then they can be together."

Leaf pushed her away and walked toward his walk-in closet. "Let's cross that bridge when we get there," he responded, fully prepared to veto her decision at that time.

****

Bethany sat in the passenger seat of Nine's black Phantom Coupe, Samantha was in the back and the energy Nine exuded upon both of them was intense. As she steered the car quietly toward Victory's house she hadn't blinked once, causing the sisters to stir with fear.

Both wondered were the rumors true?

Was Nine Prophet capable of murder?

Against her own people?

"I'm sorry, Nine," Bethany started, her smile lifting only on one side of her face. "I didn't mean—"

"He is a man, cousin," Nine said cutting her off, eyes never leaving the road. "He is a man and yet both of you fight over him as if he is immortal. As if there is no other."

"There is no other available Prophet," Samantha responded. "Their marriage means I'm alone. Who can I marry out of purity? You have Leaf, mother has Blake. What about me?" Her head drooped. "And I know you're angry, but it wasn't even as bad as it seemed," she whispered. "We were talking about him on the way back from getting her dress. All I did was explain that the only reason he was marrying her instead of me was because of her looks." She turned her head toward the window and caught a reflection of her face. "That he clearly enjoys spending more time with me because we're always together."

"And then I told her I was pregnant," Bethany said rubbing her belly. "With me and Noel's first child." Suddenly she grew angry. "So she hit me and I defended myself."

Nine looked into Bethany's eyes and then down at her flat belly. Although she understood the rules of their family, Bethany's pregnancy came at the most inopportune time for the wine venture.

Silence.

"Oh, Nine, aren't you happy for me?" Bethany sang, eyes wide with excitement. "Say something because your silence is killing me."

"You are sisters. Circumstances may make it appear otherwise but at the end of the day, you are sisters. Even the Romans who practiced blood purity remained cordial if one was chosen over the other. Why must we display ourselves so poorly in front of outsiders, when we are already being judged?"

Silence.

The sisters dropped their heads.

"Now, the wedding is off until next year, pending an investigation with the airline," Nine continued. "You are being charged as terrorists! Do you not see what the fuck you have done wrong? This is why grandfather was so strict and so rigid! This entire family is falling apart."

Both women looked at Nine in shock because she rarely used profanity. Believing they didn't care or understand why this was so important to her, she pulled the car over. "Get out."

"Excuse me?" Bethany said.

"I said get out of my car." She looked at both of them. "I do not want to see you two for awhile. Please understand that it will be best for you and me. I can be homicidal when angry and that is a side neither of you want to see."

Frightened, they opened the door and Nine pulled off, running over Samantha's foot in the process.

Her cries of pain didn't stop Nine from getting away from the scene. She didn't even look in the rearview mirror to see if she was okay. Any and everything was getting on her nerves. So when her phone rang, she snatched it up and said, "This better not be bad news."

"Okay, I'll call back later," a woman said.

Frowning, she asked, "Who is this?"

"It's Shawna, Gene's...I mean Galileo's baby mother."

Nine rolled her eyes and slammed her hand on the steering wheel. "What is wrong? Is his child okay?"

"I lost my job two weeks ago and Galileo hasn't brought by child support in weeks. So the baby and me are hungry. Ms. Nine, I'm sorry to bother you but anything you can do to help us will be appreciated."

****

Galileo was on the court playing a pick up game of basketball with a few of his young sidekicks. It was his day off so he figured after shooting some hoops he would go meet Banker, and see how wet she could really get. Besides, it had been a few days since he last laid dick on her. But right now, he had to win the game.

Dribbling the basketball toward the hoop, he was going for the layup when someone from his right blocked his shot hard. Preventing him from making the basket. He was about to bark on him until he saw it was Antonius, and when he turned to his right he was smacked in the face by Nine before she tugged one of his ears and pulled him toward an all black six-passenger van.

Four of her men accompanied her.

As Galileo made the involuntary trip, his heart beat rapidly as his friends erupted into laughter. With pointed fingers and covered mouths, he had unwillingly become their entertainment for the day. Nine had made a fool of him and if nothing else, he vowed to make her pay.

After being driven to Shawna's house, the van parked and the door flew opened. Nine appeared and said, "Get out."

He obeyed with a tough push to the back by Antonius. Men followed him as if he were a prisoner and about to be executed, with Nine in the lead. When they made it to Shawna's door she opened it and stepped back to let them inside. She was a pretty dark-skinned girl with hazel eyes and a loving smile.

The furniture inside the tiny house was old but everything was neat and clean. Toys lined the wall but there wasn't a thing out of place. It was obvious that she was a good mother and Nine wondered what she saw in Galileo that she would allow him to enter her body.

"Come inside," she greeted everyone. "Please." She allowed them inside and felt the heat Galileo was giving her.

His face was contorted with rage until Nine said, "There is no need in being angry with her. This is all your fault."

"See what you did?" he asked looking over at Shawna. "You got my fucking boss involved. This embarrassing!"

"I needed the money, G! You don't know what it's like going to school and having to pay for daycare when you make minimum wage. Since you won't help me build a life for your child, I have to do it on my own. So I need an education. What's wrong with that?"

He waved her off. "Shut the fuck up. You just another gold digging ass bitch. Just like the rest."

Shawna started to smack him but Nine stopped her.

"You are as sad as they come," Nine said. "Nothing like your father." She looked at Shawna and softened her stare. "Where is your son?"

"In the back." She paused, still being held hostage by the evil of Galileo's words. Focusing on the hallway, she said, "Denarius, come! Your father is here."

Nine and her men readjusted their dispositions as to not scare the child. Like magic, they removed their judgmental stares off of Galileo and smiled, each preparing to see the kid. Within seconds, the cutest little boy Nine had ever seen since Julius came zipping out of the room. His chocolate skin and large eyes complimented by extra long lashes made him adorable enough to want to steal.

Having seen his father a few times, he ran up to him and wrapped his little arms around one of Galileo's legs. Still mad he was yanked off of the basketball court, at first he didn't acknowledge the kid. Treated him like a nigga off the street. That was, until he was met with a hard smack to the back of his head, out of the child's view. With the sudden inspiration, he rubbed his dome and said, "Hey, lil nigga." His statement was as dry as a bag of uncooked rice.

Shawna saw his loveless attitude, rolled her eyes and said, "Go on back and play, Denarius."

Obeying his mother, he hugged his father again and rolled out.

Nine stepped in front of Galileo. And although she was about to address Shawna, her gaze remained on him. "Shawna, this man is incapable of being a father."

"How you figure?" He frowned.

"Anybody who could look down at that child and not even smile is worthless." She paused. And then, thinking of her own father, said, "I do not know how men can bring children into this world and treat them as an afterthought. But I will say this; you will take care of your responsibilities. That child is Jameson's grandson and I will not allow you to mess up his life just because you can." She stepped closer and her men covered her. "Empty your pockets."

Slowly he removed all of the cash he had on him and dropped it on Shawna's table. It totaled a little over a thousand dollars. Nine cleared her purse and in the end, Shawna had $4,500 in cash.

"You are fired, Gene," Nine barked addressing him by his birth name and not the honorable name she'd given him. "Don't come back to the academy."

Suddenly he felt something in his hardened heart. Now all of a sudden he had emotions. Too bad they were for his own self. "Why?" he asked with wide eyes. "What I lose my job for?"

"Because you have no honor. And a man without honor cannot be trusted."

****

Lately, Nine had not been feeling well both physically and mentally, but still there was much to do. Like the meeting with her board to discuss the drug operation and the brewing trouble with the Russian Cartel.

Nine, the head of the conclave, stood up and looked at the men before her. Unlike her soldiers who were vicious with weapons and fists, the men before her were experienced in the mental department. They were Mox, Riley, her cousin Noel and her uncle Blake.

From the beef with the Russians by way of the Kennedy Kings, to in-house issues pertaining to a few disloyal lieutenants, tonight's agenda was pregnant with issues that needed resolving.

Dressed in designer suits and serious miens, the men awaited their young leader's word. "First, I would like to apologize for calling you in on your day off. I understand that before my grandfather died there was an agreement to honor your personal time twice a week. Unfortunately, today I need you."

"Don't worry about that," Mox said as he scratched his salt and pepper hair. He worked with Kerrick at the onset of his career in the drug business and had been with him ever since. This was during the age when Kerrick was a dope boy and far from a drug mogul. "If there is one thing that can be said about you it is that you're fair. So if we're here, it must be for a reason."

She smiled and nodded before walking slowly around the table, with her hands clasped behind her back. "I just received word from Antonius that two of our trusted men were murdered late last night. And seeing as how our peers, the Kennedys, alerted us of impending doom, I take it that this hit was attributed to the Russians."

"So what's the plan for retaliation?" Riley, another one of Kerrick's long time friends, asked. He rubbed his baldhead before clasping his hands before him on the table. "Because this matter requires tact and caution. If the Russians are involved, they have the potential to put serious dents into our business."

She nodded in agreement. "I understand, which is why we must brace ourselves for war. And I assembled you all here today to solicit your advice."

"Do we know what sparked this attack?" Noel asked.

"From what I am told, the Russians want direct contact with Mitch and the Kennedys are refusing to give them access. By attacking Mitch's main clientele, for instance the Prophets, they're hoping to impact his business."

"Why is that?" Mox asked.

"I do not have all of the facts. But what I am told is that the Russians received their coke by way of the Kennedys," Nine explained. "At a fair price. However, this is unlike the business relationship we have earned with Mitch, which gives us a direct connection." She paused. "The Russians do not want to go through the Kennedys anymore. And I believe the Kennedys feel disrespected in the Russians' attempt to bypass them to get through to Mitch."

"So basically the Russians are trying to snatch up Mitch," Mox said.

"Thereby corning the drug market," Riley responded.

"Exactly," Nine said. "If this happens, either we will be forced to deal with the Russians, because I am sure they will kill Mitch and gain access to his cocaine crops, or we will have to find another connect with lower quality product."

The men grumbled.

"What are the Kennedys suggesting?" Mox asked.

"That we combine forces and take out the Russians," she explained. "Apparently, the Russians have connected with Vito Gambino of the Gambino family out of New York, Derrick Reaper from New Jersey and Jim Rabiu, an African from California."

The men all looked at one another. "Not sure about the others but Derrick has about one hundred men who are called the Reapers at his disposal," Mox explained.

"Although they don't have anywhere near the amount of men we do, their most dangerous weapon is Larry," Riley interjected. "He's a young thug who knows how to kill well. With him alive, it could be more problems than we need."

"Yeah, he's worth five hundred of our men alone," Mox added.

"Some of our soldiers are still getting their skills up on weaponry," Jameson added. "They won't be ready for him without more experience at this stage."

Nine sat on the edge of the table and looked at her men. "My grandfather chose right by having you all on his council. And now I rely on your advice. Should we lend assistance to the Kennedys or stand down from this war?"

The men looked at one another. "I think we should stay out of it," Noel suggested.

"Me too," Blake responded.

"And if we do, what will we risk? What will I risk as the leader?"

"Nothing in the beginning," Mox advised. "You command an army of about a thousand men, way more than the Kennedys could hope for. With a little guidance and longer hours of training, we could take out the Reapers eventually. But in the future, you will lose what may be considered more valuable."

"Which is?" she asked.

"Your respect in the industry," Mox said. "Your respect amongst your peers for not fighting. And your respect amongst your men."

"And depending on what you hold important, to some that may mean everything," Riley added.

Nine contemplated what they were saying when suddenly everyone in the room began to laugh at her. With a scowl on her face, she asked, "What's so funny? Did I miss something?"

The laughter grew louder and within seconds, their faces contorted in large circles. It was as if their eyes drifted behind their heads to make way for their unusually large mouths. "I asked what are you laughing at?" she yelled louder. "This is unprofessional! What is so funny?"

Confused at Nine's disposition, they stood up and approached her. "Are you okay, Nine?"

When she ended that call, another came in from ̶onius. "Hello."

"I have bad news," he said. "Should it wait?"

She sighed, wanting to say yes. "What is it?"

"Shawna, Galileo's baby mama, has been killed." He paused. "And the little boy may have to go into the foster care system because he doesn't have anywhere to go."

She fell back into the seat, partially defeated. "She did not have any parents?"

"She had no one." He paused. "I can have my daughter look after him for a little while until we figure out what to do."

"If you do not mind, that would be great. I need some time to think." She paused. "And find Gene."

"Want me to take care of it when I do?"

"No, just keep an eye on him but remain out of sight. I want him to think he is not a suspect, or that I do not even know about it."

She knew Galileo had everything to do with the murder and she had no respect for him. She had plans to handle him but now was not the time. At the moment, she had to see about her crazy cousin.

When the car parked, Nine's soldier opened the door and she rushed out to see what had Victory so angry she was losing her mind. Before she made it into her aunt's home, she heard, "Hello, Nine Prophet! Aren't you beautiful today!"

When Nine looked up to see where the voice was coming from she saw her cousin Isabel standing on a rod outside of her bedroom window, four stories high. Her bare feet pressing against the iron as if she were walking a tightrope sideways. If she fell, she would surely slam down on the concrete outside of her house and morph into a bloody pulp. "Isn't it a beautiful day?"

Nine's heart dropped as she witnessed the scene but she remained calm. At first, she thought Victory was exaggerating but now she knew everything she said was true. Isabel Prophet, at the moment, appeared delirious.

She backed against the wall in fear of the demons. "Get away from me! Do you hear me? Get away!"

****

The sheets were pulled up under Nine's chin as she lay in bed, unsure if she was experiencing reality or a dream. Chipo got word in Africa from Leaf that Nine had suffered a mental breakdown and she called twenty times to check on her wellbeing. But each time, Nine refused to answer, because she didn't know what to say. If she wasn't calling, then the nobles were and as much as she relied on their strength, even they were bothers.

What was wrong with her?

Was she going mad?

Alone in her bedroom for the moment, she was sure that it wouldn't last.

The meeting last night was a wreck and she was dismal, unable to make a move. How embarrassing it was to perform so strangely in front of the Nobles. And as much as she begged for privacy, Leaf would not leave her be. His concern was pushy and borderline irritating but she knew he loved her; it was evident in his eyes as he asked, "What's wrong, bae? Talk to me."

As she thought, slowly Leaf opened the door and walked into his dark bedroom. Married to her for a little over a year, he learned never to turn on lights if she had them off. It either meant she was resting or contemplating her troubles.

Slowly Leaf eased into the bed and sat up against the headboard. Not wanting to be bothered at first, the moment she smelled the faint scent of his expensive cologne, she wiggled closer to him and laid her head into the center of his lap. "Am I crazy, cousin? Do you think that somehow, despite my best efforts, I have gone mad?"

"Never."

"Then why is it that lately everything that has been happening to me makes me think that I am not of this world? Once, I had things under control, and now..."

"I don't know, bae. But I do know together we will find out. Whatever has sparked your change of mental state is right in front of us. We just have to find it."

CHAPTER TWI

"Two of thy whelps, fell curs of blc
- **William Shakespeare**

Nine sat in the back of her Maybach pressed against her ear. These days more calls than the president of the United Sta

The caller of the moment was Banker. "I kn believe me but I swear on everything I love, I v there but I was sick. By the time I got up for v already five hours late so I just stayed home."

"What about me makes you think that I am stu paused. "That I would believe such nonsense? Wha please tell me, Banker, so that I can remedy it now."

"It isn't you I just…"

"Wanted to be under your boyfriend instead of rep for work," she said cutting her off. She looked out window just as her car pulled up to Victory's house. "I v sure like to meet the boy who has taken all of your tim needed you today, Banker. There are things that are go on with me and I needed you here. I expect you to cor tomorrow with no excuses."

"I will be there," she said, her voice heavy with irritation "Before I go, I wanted to remind you about my trip to Aruba for two weeks. I'll be leaving soon."

"I remember," Nine said plainly, relieved some of her mental faculties were still in place. "We will talk about everything else later. In the meantime, did you contact Bambi Kennedy?"

"Yes. I told her you would be attending the dinner at her home. She said she'd have a car pick you up at around eight. Something about the location being off the grid and you wouldn't find it without it. She also told me to tell you not to worry. That the driver will take you back home the moment you're ready."

"Good. I will speak with you later."

Just…like…her.

"Isabel, what are you doing up there?" Nine asked. "Are you feeling well?"

"As well as I can be," she yelled. "I'm trying to convince my mother that I can fly but she doesn't believe me." She extended her arms out along the sides of her body as if she were a plane. "Tell me something, cousin, do you?"

Nine searched Isabel's eyes. Isabel and Nine didn't spend much time together but she felt they connected on a personal level. Even during the most extreme situation, she could feel it.

Nine grinned and said, "Isabel, I believe you can do anything you want. So let me see you do it, cousin." She paused. "Jump and I will be down here waiting," she continued, calling her bluff.

Isabel giggled.

Finally, she met someone as crazy as she was.

****

Nine walked into the sitting room, which was directly off of the living room in her mansion. She plopped down next to Isabel who was lying down on the sofa, having just gotten up from a nap. The room was decorated in expensive gold-trimmed furniture that was extremely comforting and peaceful.

"How was your nap?" Nine asked. "I would have taken you to one of the other rooms but the moment you sat down on this sofa, you drifted off to sleep."

Isabel sat up straight and rubbed her head. "I was thinking about going to a room but the banging from the construction workers made my head rattle. So I stayed where I was. What are you building?"

"Just some additions I need to make my home complete," Nine responded.

"How did you know I wouldn't jump?"

"I believe you would have. Before I got there. But the curiosity of my statement interested you. So you could not die until you found out why."

She giggled realizing she was on to her. "Is it true that grandfather hurt you?" Isabel asked staring at the walls. "That he made you have sex with him and then beat you for it?" She looked over at Nine, waiting for an answer.

Would she be forthcoming or closed and stuffy as Alice made her appear to be?

She exhaled. "It is partially true," Nine said folding her legs on the top of the couch in a lotus position. "He did not make love to me during the beatings. It was not until after my freedom. Although he never told me, something about how he looked at me, as if he were looking through me, made me feel he wanted more from me. I fear he may have never given me my freedom if I did not give him my body. But it was my choice."

Isabel took a moment to observe the pictures in the room. They were all members of her family, even her cousins Lydia and Paige, Nine's sisters, who were dead.

Finally, her gaze settled on something that took her breath away. It was a portrait that sat on the wall boldly as if it were more important than the other photos. "Who is that?" She turned around and looked at Nine. "She looks like," she focused on the picture again, "you."

"I only wish," Nine said modestly. "Her name is Thandi and she was grandfather's first wife," she sighed. "She was the only woman he ever loved."

"More than grandmother?"

"The love he had for Thandi did not come close to how he felt for grandmother," Nine admitted.

"So he loved you as deeply as he loved her," Isabel responded.

Nine smiled.

"What happened in this house? Between you and Cousin Alice?"

Nine sighed. "Some people are sexually aroused by controlling others. Alice is that kind of person. I do not even think it is a bad thing. How we are raised determines our personalities. But she is different. Evil. I never told anybody this, not even my husband, but she used to beat me and make me please her sexually. I never forgave her for how mean she was about it."

"And you let her live?"

"Alice and I have our date with destiny planned," Nine assured her. "She doesn't know when. However, I do."

"I think you should be careful. Alice is capable of many things."

Nine giggled. "So am I."

Silence.

"Enough of the others. What is going on with you, Isabel? Honestly?"

"I don't know," she shrugged. "I mean…sometimes I feel together, and even hopeful about my mental stability. Like each day will be different than the last. Most times I worry though…mostly about what kind of angry I'll be. Little angry or big angry," she said opening her arms. "I also worry about hurting people. I never want to bring my wrath down on someone innocent."

Sounds like me, Nine thought.

"My father used to rape me and allow other men to rape me too." Isabel's eyes widened as she stared into the room. "But after awhile, I decided that would stop. And every now and again, when I'm alone, flashes of those days come back. I will never let anyone rape me again though, I'm sure of that."

Nine understood what it meant to be used and she made mental notes to fire Blake's ass from her team in the morning. Any man who would take advantage of his own daughter was not noble and she wanted him far away from her business. "How did you stop it?"

"Easily," she grinned. "I simply let the last man get good and comfortable inside of me. Where it's nice and warm." She raised her dress with one hand and rubbed her breast with the other. "And when he was about to get to that special place," she stuffed her finger into her vagina, "then I pulled the knife from under my pillow and cut his dick off." She looked over at Nine, removed her finger from her body and fixed her clothing. "See…it's easy." Her head lowered in shame. "Sorry, I've been known to go too far. Hope I didn't offend you."

Nine was fascinated by her sexual deviancy. "Can you control your mind sometimes? Because when I am around you, you always seem so collected. I would never know something was off with you."

"Yes. I can control myself quite well. If my feelings aren't hurt." She thought about her broken friendship with Alice, which sparked her recent episodes.

"How?"

"I just make myself cum."

With raised eyebrows, she asked, "And that works?"

"Every time," she grinned. "Are you going to put me away, Nine? Mama says I can't live with her anymore, although I can come to visit. She said she doesn't want me being responsible for doing something crazy and ruining your wine venture. She's even given Alice my room. But now I don't care if I ever go back."

"You are free to live here, with me. I have plenty of space."

Isabel was shocked. She never dreamed she'd be so close to the most powerful person in the family. "Thank you." She looked into her eyes. "Do you think I'm crazy?"

"If you are, it is because they made you that way." She paused and touched her face. "They made *us* that way. But at least now, we have each other."

****

Nine sat in the backseat of a sedan that Bambi Kennedy commissioned to pick her and Leaf up for the important meeting. Although the Russian business initially was not a problem for the Prophets, conveniently for the Kennedys, now it was.

Nine hoped she'd be okay at the meeting, as far as her sanity was concerned, but after she had a glass of wine earlier, mentally she was feeling off. Had it been a meeting of less importance, she would've rescheduled but she didn't have that honor.

Once Nine and Leaf arrived, they were taken to a door leading to a secluded luxury bunker. Although the Kennedys resided there at the moment, it wasn't their real home. They were in hiding and had the property built to go underground during perilous times. Considering the beef with the Russians, the time was now.

When the butler opened the door to the bunker, Nine nodded and smiled at him. The collar of her black fur coat stroked Nine's high cheekbones and set off her gorgeous dark skin. The butler stepped back and allowed her inside where she was greeted by the stunning Bambi Kennedy.

Upon first sight, Nine was taken aback by Bambi's beauty. The long black dress she wore made way for her brown thigh and her hair sat on the top of her head in a sexy bun.

She looked like anything other than a drug lord.

When Nine glanced inside, she was also impressed at how beautiful the other Kennedy family members were. The Prophets and the Kennedys rarely made outside appearances so this was the first time they were meeting each other.

Scarlett, wife to Camp Kennedy, had her red hair hanging over her shoulder and brushing against the straps of the black silk dress that she wore. Bradley Kennedy's wife Denim's dreads were pulled in a neat ponytail while Race, wife to Ramirez Kennedy, wore her hair in a sharp bob that hung at her jawbone.

The fellas were equally attractive, dipped in designer business suits and casual gear.

"Bambi, it's a pleasure to finally meet you," Nine said with a slight nod and smile.

Bambi was impressed that Nine appeared to possess the qualities of a queen. "The pleasure is all mine," Bambi said softly. "The circumstances aren't the best but I'm glad you could make it."

"What better circumstance than war?" she winked.

"You have a beautiful home," Leaf said politely, walking behind Nine. He handed Bambi a bottle of Ace of Spades, even though she requested the guests bring only themselves, and Bambi thought the move was classy.

"Thank you," Bambi replied. "My sister will show you to your seats," she responded as Denim approached with a smile.

Nine and Leaf took their seats and waited as the other bosses trickled inside. They were Rasim and Snow Nami of the Nami family, and Carissa, Mercedes and Yvette, who were affectionately called Pitbulls in a Skirt. Also there was Lil C, Mercedes' son, and lastly Kelsi who was born in the dope game and used to move coke with his mother Janet.

With everyone present, Bambi swaggered over to the table. She was preparing to thank them for coming when a large woman walked out of the back of the house. She posted next to Nine and she could smell the alcohol stemming from her skin.

Obviously drunk out of her mind, she said, "I'm sick of you bitches not inviting me to the party. With all these fine ass niggas in here." She eyeballed Kelsi, Rasim, Leaf and Lil C. "I'm a part of this family too, you know?"

She slithered her tongue into the cup and lapped at the wine while looking at Bambi through the bottom of the glass. It was obvious that she was trying to irritate her and she was doing a good job.

Bambi was headed over toward her but Kevin got up and placed his palm on Bambi's lower back. "I got her, baby." He kissed her on the cheek and ushered her away.

"Sorry for the distraction," Bambi said addressing the group. "Let's eat and then do as bosses do."

When dinner was over and cocktails were served, Nine decided to get right down to business. "Where is Mitch?" she asked referring to her drug connect. She leaned back in the chair with her legs crossed. "Shouldn't he be present at this meeting?"

"He should, but considering that security is high, we feel it best to keep him out of it," Kevin responded.

"Besides, we're all grown," Bambi joked. "We don't need daddy."

"So you don't trust us?" Leaf responded.

"We're in the dope business," Bambi replied. "Where the motto is trust no one."

They all smiled.

"And yet you invite us to your home anyway," Nine winked at Bambi.

"Trust is one thing," Bambi explained. "Respect is another. Which you earned."

Nine nodded and winked again and Bambi liked her even more. They were each other's woman crush.

"Tell me something, what makes you think the Russians will try to take out our entire operation?" Kelsi questioned as he wiped his hand down his chin. "It seems a little ambitious."

"Because the hope is that if your operations are down, you won't have money to cop coke from Mitch," Denim said.

"And if you don't have money, Mitch isn't eating the same way he has in the past and his profits will be down," Bradley added. "So they're trying to smoke Mitch out to force him to do business with them."

"But if they can't get Mitch, why impact *our* businesses?" Yvette asked. "We don't buy from the Russians."

"Because eventually the Russians hope to bully you into a business relationship with them, using whatever bullshit product they secure," Kevin responded.

While they began to talk, Nine started to feel loopy again. Suddenly black figures appeared to surround everyone and their bodies looked stretched like rubber bands. Remembering what Isabel said, she leaned over to Leaf and whispered, "Finger me."

He looked at her as if she was crazy…and at the moment, she was. "Now?" he asked through clenched teeth.

"It's my mind," she said softly.

Not knowing how a bout of delirium could be reduced by an orgasm, for the love of his wife, he was willing to try anything. So he snaked his hand under the table, beneath her dress and through the slickness of her warm pussy. To other guests it looked as if his hand was on her thigh but it was anywhere but.

Slowly he stroked her clit and brought her attention to the pleasure, not the strange shapes of their bodies. The crazy thoughts didn't disappear.

Nine's pussy was drenched and although the figures before her still looked weird, she went with it. She was embracing whatever crazy effect was taking over her mind in the moment. "Let us say the Russians do want war," Nine said bringing everyone back to the meeting at hand. "And let us say they try to dismantle our operations if we refuse to use their coke. What is your plan?"

Leaf started playing with her pussy a little too good, causing her to grip at the napkins in front of her.

"Yeah, why we here?" Kelsi asked.

"You're here because the Russians have connected with other bosses," Bambi said. "Together they are calling themselves the Russian Cartel and they command a big army. I was hoping that we could do the same. Combine our soldiers and fight back. Together, we are legion."

Nine smiled, realizing her comment was a play on her organization's name.

"And where's Mitch again?" Rasim questioned.

"We have him held up for his protection," Bambi responded. "Once we deal with the Russian Cartel, then we'll let him go. But don't worry, while we have him in custody, business will still move as usual. Bricks are still being sold."

"And how does one deal with the Russian Cartel?" Snow asked.

"We kill them," Bambi responded.

Silence.

Nine smiled and said, "War is a necessary evil."

Bambi nodded, never getting enough of Nine. "Yes it is, friend."

"So when do you think they will make a move?" Nine asked.

"One of their fiancés was murdered today. The order was given by us in response to the men they killed in our organizations. We also took out their best soldier. A man by the name of Larry. And I'm sure because of it, they're angry and disabled." Bambi paused. "I reason that they'll make another move on your camps any day now."

"Well if they do," Nine said with a smile on her face, "we will be ready."

"So are you all in?" Bambi looked around the table. "Because I need an answer tonight. Can I see a show of hands?"

Believing his wife was okay at the moment, Leaf eased his fingers out of her wet pussy and wiped the excess juice on a dinner napkin. Thanks to her, his dick was rock hard and he wondered if it would go down in time.

Starting with Nine Prophet, one by one, the bosses raised their hands. In the Kennedy family, Race was the first followed by everyone else.

Bambi appeared relieved. "Thank you," Bambi said to everyone. "As you know, I invited you all to stay here in the bunker tonight and I hope that you will take me up on my offer. In the event the war is extra bloody, you and your families are welcome to come here for protection. This place is off the grid to everyone, including the police."

Nine stood up and Leaf went to grab her fur coat from the butler. "I appreciate the offer, friend, but my husband and I have a war to plan for in the privacy of our own home." She strolled over to Bambi and she reminded Bambi of Cleopatra.

Strong, bold and elegant.

"Do not worry about us," Nine continued. "We will be ready for them." She extended her hand. "It is such a pleasure to be in the company of a real king. A real woman. I look forward to doing more business with you in the future."

Bambi shook her delicate hand. "Same here."

Once they were outside, Leaf said, "How do you feel? In your mind?"

"Still crazy," she responded. "Something is going on with me and I do not know what."

"So what do you think about the meeting?"

"I think Bambi is great. I also think she killed a few of our men to get us to align with her."

Leaf was surprised. With widened eyes, he asked, "And you okay with that?"

"They were problem soldiers and I believe she knew that. They were men I did not respect who were bound to be cut anyway. So why would I not be okay with a woman who did something I would have done myself? If anything, I respect her even more." She looped her arm through his.

****

Nine and Gates sat in her backyard looking at her vineyard. When he gazed over at her he noticed that she didn't look the same. "What has life given you that you can't handle?"

She giggled. "The reason you ask?"

"Because every time I see you, you are put together. But now, well, now you look uneven. Unkempt. Why?"

Nine observed him. For a second she contemplated telling him her real reasons, that her mind had gone awry but it wasn't relevant information to give him. He wasn't a doctor. "I have a few things going on in my life. But I am Nine Prophet. And there is nothing I cannot handle with a little time."

Gates nodded, sensing her hesitation to be truthful.

She pulled up the collar of her jacket. "I asked you to come here because I cannot see you anymore."

His eyebrows rose. "Why?"

"Out of respect for my husband. He loves me and I need to love him back."

"And you don't?"

"I mean the right way. At first, I thought he was cheating but now I know he just needs time."

He sighed and removed his phone from his pocket. He pushed a few keys, scrolled a few times and handed her his phone. "I didn't want to show you this but you've left me no other choice." He paused. "This woman is bound to be the source of a problem if you don't handle her."

Nine removed the phone from his hand and looked down at the pictures on the screen. She blinked a few times to clear her vision and when she was done, she could clearly see her husband with a strange but beautiful woman. His hands were on her shoulders and he was staring intently into her eyes.

Now that Nine recalled, it was the same woman who was at the Royal Babies event.

Did she come to blow up her husband's spot? By telling her that they were together?

In a low whisper and with a quivering chin, she asked, "Who is she?" She stared up at Gates.

"Keep scrolling," he responded. "And then you tell me what it looks like."

With each swipe, Nine witnessed her husband on different days with the same woman. Her stomach bubbled and she tossed the phone into his lap and paced the area in front of him. "Why would you show me something like that?" She stopped. "When you yourself said I looked unkempt?" She paused. "Did you do it to hurt me?"

"I figured this was the reason you were upset, Nine. I wasn't trying to—"

"Ruin my marriage?" She waited. "Get out of my house, Sir Gates!"

"But—"

"I am being polite now," she said as she turned her head so that she faced the vineyard instead of his face. "But the next time, you will consider me and my men rude."

When Gates spun around, six of Nine's soldiers had already descended on him. Although they didn't pull their weapons, he knew if he didn't leave, things would escalate so he stood up, buttoned his suit jacket and walked away.

CHAPTER THIRTEEN

"What signifies my deadly-standing eye, My silence and my cloudy melancholy."
- William Shakespeare

Alice stood in front of her aunts and uncles in Victory's living room, pleading her case. After so much plotting and planning, she was officially able to get their attention. After the Samantha and Bethany scandal, Nine tightened her grip on the funds. Although she didn't cut them completely off, as she threatened at the family dinner, she stopped taking their calls about extra money.

Things only heightened when Samantha's foot was broken due to Nine running over it.

Victory, Marina, Noel and Blake were all present.

"Alice, this is very risky," Victory said. "You are making huge accusations when there's no proof to your claim."

"I beg to differ. Including the fact that she ran over Samantha's foot with her car, we have even more," Alice said looking at Blake and Noel. "Don't we?" she continued, referring to the information she got about Nine zapping out at a Prophet meeting from Noel and Blake.

"Even if she is crazy like you say, most of the Prophet fortune is made illegally," Blake said. "How can we even be sure what is our due?"

"It doesn't matter," Alice continued. "I contacted grandfather's old accountant who still keeps Nine's books. He says she's placed all of the money into the account via legal entities. Her biggest fear after Leaf was arrested last year was the feds coming down on her and finding stacks of cash in her possession. She's too smart for her own good. If we get a hold of the accounts, we get control of every penny. All five hundred million dollars of it!"

Their jaws dropped. "She has that much money in the bank?" Victory yelled. "And the bitch won't let me hold $100,000?"

"Fuck that!" Marina yelled. "At least you get extra money from her every other week, outside of the allotments. I only get what she sends once a month. She never gives me more even when I beg." Frown lines possessed her face. "And now I'm hearing she has close to a billion?"

"She trims off your amount because you on drugs!" Blake reminded her.

Alice tried to conceal her excitement at how angry her family was. Their rage was intoxicating. "I've been telling you she doesn't belong on the Prophet throne. Bethany and Samantha need a defense team and now we have to rely on her mood for money?" She paused. "It's not fair."

"So what do we have to do?" Marina asked, eager to get more cash for more dope.

"I met with a lawyer who says based on the information I gave him, that we have a case," she explained. "All we have to do is get some harder evidence to convince the court that she's crazy." She paused. "Then he'll submit a motion and subpoena to freeze access to the bank accounts. If everyone in the family votes, we can have her removed as head of the estate. With the majority of Prophets on our side, we can control how the money is distributed." She looked at all of them. "Are you in?"

Silence.

"I hope I don't live to regret this," Victory said. "But I'm in."

One by one the others raised their hands, sealing their fates.

CHAPTER FOURTEEN

"Why dost not comfort me, and help me out from this
unhallowed and blood-stained hole?"
- William Shakespeare

The music played softly as Leaf steered his black
Porsche along the road leading into Aristocrat Hills.
For the past few days, Nine had been avoiding him and he
didn't know why. Earlier he decided to take a break from the
mansion and went to the bar to get a few drinks but no
matter what he did, he couldn't shake her from his mind.

He loved Nine.

But her nonchalant attitude about their marriage was
taking its toll. Not only that, but he was tiring of the time she
spent with Gates even though, to his knowledge, she hadn't
seen him in the past few days.

Something was certainly off in his marriage and he had to
resolve it before it was too late. They came too far to end like
this. The plan was to go in the house and have the maid,
who just returned from sick leave, cook dinner. Then he
would have a serious conversation with her.

When he raised the electronic remote, which opened the
large iron gate with the word PROPHET scrawled into the
pattern, he took a deep breath. A few seconds later, he saw
what looked to be his wife walking down the street naked
holding their child.

Was he losing his mind?

He blinked a few times, believing he was tripping but to
no avail. Nine was as nude as the day she was born and her
eyes were so bugged that you could barely see the browns of
her pupils.

He whipped his car on the side of the road, hopped out
and approached her with extreme urgency. Julius was crying
at the top of his lungs and when he rushed in front of her,
she attempted to move around him, her gaze remaining on
the horizon. It was as if she didn't recognize him.

"Nine, what's going on?" She continued to push forward so he blocked her step, removed the baby from her arms and yelled, "What the fuck is going on, bae?" He got up in her face. "Talk to me!"

"Mrs. Prophet, Mrs. Prophet," Banker yelled coming down the hill with a robe in her hand. "Please put this on!"

When Leaf saw her assistant, he was partially relieved because now he would have help. She walked up to him and he said, "Take the baby back to the house, Banker." He snatched the robe and handed her the infant. "What happened to Nine?" He placed it on his wife's body. "Why is she out here like this?"

"I don't know," she responded shivering. "One moment she was watching TV and drinking wine. The next thing I knew, she was yelling about people coming to get her and that she was too hot." Her eyes widened and she covered her mouth with her hands. "Mr. Lincoln, I'm scared to work for her anymore," she yelled putting on a performance. "I don't know what to do!"

He put his hand on her shoulder. "Don't be afraid, Banker. I need your help right now. Just take care of my son and I'll talk about your future with us. Possibly even a raise. Okay?"

She nodded yes.

"Good, now take Julius in. I'll be along in a minute." She didn't move. "Don't be scared. Just go now."

Banker finally walked up the hill toward the house with the infant in her arms.

With his son safe, Leaf turned around to get a hold of Nine who walked a yard or so out. Instead of speaking to her, he picked her up and tossed her over his shoulder. He moved toward his Porsche, placed her inside and eased back into the driver's seat before she could contest.

As he kicked the car into drive, he gazed over at her periodically, wishing the strange-acting woman was anyone else but his wife. Placing a hand on her thigh, he said, "Baby, what's going on?" His voice cracked and for a second he felt like less than a man for sounding so weak.

Was he about to cry?

But the pain he was feeling from not being able to assist his wife could no longer disguise itself. "Let me help you!" He paused. "Please!"

****

"You do not understand, someone is trying to kill me, Leaf!" Nine yelled. She was standing in the middle of the living room; a soft pink robe covered her body. "Look at him! He is there! He is over there!"

Leaf turned his head in the direction of her finger, knowing all the while that nothing was there. Besides, he looked in the same area twenty times earlier and never saw a figure once.

Slowly he moved toward her and the moment he laid his hands on her shoulder, with wild arms she swung, slapping him in the face with her knuckles as if he was trying to hurt her and she needed to defend herself. "They're here! I need my gun because they're here! Don't you see them?"

Nine wiggled away from him and ran off to get her weapon but he wasn't concerned. Ever since she started exhibiting psychotic behavior, he removed all of the guns and put them in a safe place. Flopping down on the sofa, he tried to figure a way out of this.

He wanted to talk to someone about his troubles but couldn't go to his old friends. Prophet business was a sensitive matter that only other Prophets could understand.

But who could he trust?

When his cell phone vibrated in his pocket, he removed it and saw it was his cousin Noel. "Hey…" Leaf sounded as if the weight of the world was on his shoulders.

"What you doing right now?" Noel asked. "Trying to go to the bar to get some drinks?"

"Can't leave the house, man."

"Everything cool?"

"Nah." He paused. "Nothing's cool."

Leaf and Noel stood at the door while Nine hollered and screamed how nobody was going to harm her. Leaf's forehead was on the cool wood panel and his hand covered the doorknob as he battled with whether or not to go inside.

"How long has she been like this?"

"All day," Leaf replied. "I don't know what to do, man. If I call for help and she's committed to an institution, she'll never forgive me. I'll never forgive myself. But if she dies..."

When they heard glass break Leaf pushed the door open and rushed inside the room. Nine had broken the window with her fist and blood trickled down her arm as she attempted to jump out. Leaf rushed up to her, tore the shirt from his body and wrapped it around her wrist to slow down the bleeding. He walked her to the edge of the bed and they both sat down.

"What are you doing to yourself?" Leaf yelled, a single tear rolling down his face. He turned to Noel who already had his phone in his hand and said, "Call Doctor Banning! Now!"

CHAPTER FIFTEEN

"My heart suspects more than mine eye can see."
- William Shakespeare

Nine blinked her eyes a few times before opening them widely. When she looked up she was staring into the beautiful face of Isabel Prophet. She was sitting on one of Nine's high decorative pillows, massaging her shoulders with her warm fingertips, while humming a song that Nine was unfamiliar with.

At least the hallucinations were gone.

Pulling her pouty dry lips apart, Nine asked, "Where is Leaf?"

"He went to get you some more sleeping medicine."

"From who?"

"Dr. Banning prescribed it for you."

Nine closed her eyes before opening them again slowly. The world seemed cloudy, as if it didn't exist. When the phone rang, Isabel picked it up. "Hello?" She paused. "Hold on." She covered the receiver and said, "It's someone named Vanique from Royal Babies. She's asking for Marie Antoinette."

Reluctantly, Nine accepted the call and said, "Hello."

"I'm sorry to call you like this but Julius is out of the program!" She was rude and short.

Nine's eyes widened. "For what?"

"Two reasons! First, we found out that you lied about your name. And second, we found out that your last name is Prophet. And we don't accept incestuous behavior at our school! Goodbye!"

Nine handed her the phone. That was the last thing she felt like hearing. "Please hang it up," she said.

"Everything okay?

Nine shook her head no. "I need a bath."

"It's funny you asked. I already ran the water for you."

****
By T. Styles   139

Nine leaned back in the freestanding tub while Isabel sat on the edge of it massaging her shoulders again. "How did you learn to knead skin so smoothly?"

Isabel laughed and scratched into the row between two of her cornrows before massaging Nine's shoulders again. "My father taught me. He said the more sensual the massage, the better the orgasm."

Nine shook her head in disgust. "I fired him the other day. I am certain your parents are talking about me badly."

Isabel smiled. "Who cares? What can they do but get over it?" she shrugged. "What's wrong with you though, Nine Prophet? I haven't known you long but what has gotten your mind so racked all of a sudden? I've heard of your legend and you are always poised and subtle."

"I do not know, Isabel. I wish I did because I would put an end to it quickly. It bothers me so much that it keeps me up at night."

"Have you tried what I suggested? With giving yourself and orgasm?"

"Yes." Nine sighed. "It makes me focus on the sensations but my mind and thoughts are still the same. Wild and crazy. I feel sick lately, as if I am breaking down inside. Something else is wrong."

Isabel grabbed a washcloth, lathered it with soap and lifted Nine's arm softly to clean her pit. "Search inside, Nine." She brought the cloth to the back of her neck. "Only you know what has changed in such a short period of time. Search hard, and when you find the right answer, attack it."

Nine leaned further, while the back of her head nestled between her cousin's bear legs. "Can you make me some tea?"

"Sure. What kind?"

"Earl Grey. No sugar, no honey."

Isabel removed her feet from the tub and wrapped a large blue velvet towel around her body. "Say no more."

****

Isabel hummed all the way down the hallway toward the kitchen until she ran into Banker who was sashaying out of Julius' room. Surprised, Banker turned around and looked into Isabel's eyes as if she was caught red handed doing something wrong. "How is she doing?" Banker asked.

"Who is *she*?"

"Nine."

Isabel looked down at Banker's feet and slowly moved her gaze up to her eyes. "Do you receive a check from Nine?"

Banker flapped her lids a few times. "Excuse me?"

"Are you or are you not an employee?"

Isabel frowned, believing she already knew the answer. "I am."

"Then refer to her as Mrs. Prophet. And when you see any of us, we expect the same honor." She paused. "I believe you have something to do with Nine being sick. For your safety, I better not find out that it's true." Isabel bumped her shoulder and moved toward the kitchen as she continued her humming.

CHAPTER SIXTEEN

"I beg this boon, with tears not lightly shed."
- William Shakespeare

Nine lay in the bed, on the phone, talking to Chipo in Africa who was extremely pleased to finally hear from her. It had been weeks and she wondered how she was doing. "It has been tough," Nine admitted. "Mainly because I do not know where to begin to find out what is wrong. Dr. Banning says I am okay, and that it is probably all in my mind, but in my heart, I still feel as if something is off."

"Maybe you should go to another doctor."

Nine thought about the secrets her family possessed. The reason they continued to use Dr. Banning was because she was loyal, professional and kept Prophet business private. She couldn't say the same if she used another physician. "I just can't. With the wine venture, it's just the wrong time."

Silence.

"Nine, I want to ask you something but I need pure honesty. Can I count on you for that?"

Nine readjusted in the bed, placing more pillows behind her head. She had a feeling that what she wanted to know would be difficult for her to answer. "Of course I will, Chipo."

"Is it true? That you are from an incestuous background?"

"Yes," Nine breathed, realizing the secret was out.

"Oh, my God. What has Kerrick done to his family?"

Silence.

"What about your husband? Is he of your bloodline?"

"Yes."

Chipo exhaled. "America has ruined him."

Nine was more concerned about how Chipo felt about her than anything else. This was the moment she feared and finally it arrived. Would Chipo, whom she had grown to love, care for her the same knowing the truth? "Do you think of me differently now?"

"Of course not, dear. I'm still fond of you. Sadly, you are only a product of your environment." She paused. "But what I'm about to say is the heaviest advice I've ever given in my life. Are you prepared to hear it with an open mind?"

"Of course," she replied.

"Stop this vile lifestyle now. While you still can. Life for you will only get harder if you continue in this manner. Do not condone brothers breeding with sisters. Or cousins breeding with cousins. End your marriage and start anew while you're still young. Save your family and the generations to follow. It's the only way to break the curse."

"I cannot, Chipo. Unlike some, I do not believe that grandfather was wrong. I am smarter and stronger because of him and although my family members lose sight sometimes, I believe they are just as intelligent. Aunt Victory has four master's. Uncle Blake graduated from Harvard with a Bachelor's in Biology. Before the drugs got her, my Aunt Marina was a scientist involved in stem cell research and my husband knows several languages and is the smartest man I know," she said truthfully. "Prophet blood is more powerful because we rarely mix. Besides, all of the books I have read from the Roman era state that they participated in this type of lifestyle and they were some of the best inventors of our kind."

"But it's wrong, Nine. It's vile. Can't you see that?"

Silence.

Chipo sighed, feeling as if her words were lost on Nine. "Okay let me tell you the toughest part since you have your mind made up. For this behavior, you will pay greatly. Your family. Your children. Everyone who takes your last name. How much karmic debt you will garner will be directly related to how long you continue to lead this lifestyle." She paused. "I'm so sorry, my dear, but you have been warned."

When she hung up, feeling worse than ever, the phone rang again. She started to ignore it but she was afraid it would be more bad news and she wouldn't be able to stop it before it reached the winery. So she picked up the phone and was greeted by a woman's voice she didn't recognize. "Who is this?"

"You don't know me but I know you," the caller said.

"And what do you want?"

"Something has happened with one of the members of your family. If you handle things properly, the matter can go away with no questions asked. But if you don't, you'll have to prepare for the aftermath. I'll be in contact later with the details."

Nine slammed down the phone and placed her fingers on her forehead. Things were going from bad to worse, and she didn't see an end in sight.

Nine stood above Julius' crib, her mind sloshing and moving around like a tsunami. She was just about to pick him up when Leaf walked inside the room, strolled up behind her and snaked his arms around her waist. "How you feeling, bae?"

Nine sighed and leaned her back into his chest as she looked down at Julius. "He has to go. I am not sure when but it will have to be soon."

Leaf removed his arms and walked in front of her. Looking down at his beautiful wife, he asked, "What do you mean?"

"My mind is not right and if he stays, I fear I might hurt him, cousin. We both know it."

"Things have changed."

"How have they?"

Leaf looked down at Julius and back at his wife. "I love him too much to let him go."

Exhaling deeply, she looked into his eyes and walked away from him. Sitting on the daybed by the window, she gazed out of it and stared at the vineyard.

"I didn't think it was possible but here I am, standing before you and saying with all of my heart that I love that little nigga," Leaf said. "And I can't see anybody else taking care of him." He paused. "I'll keep him safe, Nine, don't worry. I'll keep both of you safe. Just believe in me."

Silence.

Leaf walked in front of her, knelt down and placed one hand on her thigh. "I think you may need to see another doctor. One who specializes in mental illness."

"So you do think I am crazy?"

"It's not that, Nine. It's just that, well, I don't think I can help you. I swear to God if there were one part of me that believed that I could, I wouldn't make a suggestion like this."

Her shoulders tightened. "You spoke to Chipo, did you not?"

"Yes. And she cares about you."

"Leaf, even if I wanted to get help, I cannot. Nothing is more important to me right now than this winery. I have to see Francesca through. I just have to."

Irritated, he stood up and stomped toward the window. Looking over at her, he yelled, "Why is this so important to you?"

"Does it matter?"

"After all this time, you still don't know what you mean to me." He paused. "I have given up who I am and what I believe to be with you. Do you actually think I can stand by and not see to it that you get some help?"

She was about to answer when the phone rang. She rose up, wiped her hand down her hair and in a breathy tone, asked, "Who is calling now?"

"This is Brett Jones, Attorney at Law."

Her eyebrows rose. "I believe you have the wrong number."

"No, I don't," he said confidently. "I represent the Prophet family in a case involving the estate of Kerrick Prophet."

Nine sat down on the edge of the bed. If this was the karma that Chipo spoke of, it entered her life with vengeance. "So you are saying that you are representing me in a case?"

"No," he chuckled. "I'm representing the original Prophets."

She laughed. "Sir, I am an original Prophet."

"That will be determined in court. The members I represent are the ones who were left out of your grandfather's will. Now, we are trying to come to an understanding about the estate and before this gets any further, I'd like to see if there is anything I can do to resolve this matter amicably. For instance, you stepping down from the head of Kerrick's estate."

"Why would I step down when he gave me everything?"

"That's what you say, but your family members feel differently and are willing to fight for it."

Nine swallowed and looked up into Leaf's eyes. The pain she felt as a result of the betrayal was too hard to bear. As a matter of fact, the last time she felt betrayed in this magnitude was when Fran was alive and she left her in the basement for days when she knew she was in charge of feeding her.

"You tell my family," she swallowed when the words tasted like shit in her mouth, "you tell *them* that I will fight every last one of them to the death. And when it is done, everyone involved is cut off for life."

"I'm really sorry you feel that way. You'll be hearing from me soon."

She hung up and dropped on her bed. "They are suing me." She gripped her stomach. "They are fucking suing me when all I did was try to help them!"

****

Nine sat in a large leather chair at an expensive restaurant; dark sunglasses covered most of her face because she had been crying all day and her eyes were bloodshot red.

"Baby, you have to eat something," Leaf said sitting his hand on top of hers. "You've been playing with your food. Get something in you."

Nine looked down at the steak and felt her stomach churn. "Did you make a bad decision to marry me?"

Leaf raised one brow. "Come again?"

She sighed, crossed her legs and leaned back into her seat. "I asked if you think that you made a mistake by marrying me?"

"Do me a favor, *cousin*," Leaf said sarcastically, "never disrespect me or my vows to you again. If you're mad at the family, then be mad at them but don't take it out on me. I have never left your corner. I have always been by your side."

"Are you cheating, Leaf?"

His jaw dropped. Believing she just ignored everything he said, he stood up and was about to leave until she said, "I saw her face. I saw the pictures of you with another woman. I was going to deal with it later, when I had the strength. But now I feel like I want to get all of my troubles over with altogether." She paused. "Now answer the fucking question."

Leaf sat down and looked over at her. "Bae, I'm not cheating on you."

"Then who is she? I saw pictures of you with another woman on more than one occasion. She is a beautiful red bone with brown hair. My complete opposite."

"You don't think you're beautiful?"

She pulled the sunglasses from her face and tossed them to the floor. "I asked you a question, cousin! Who is she?" she yelled slamming a fist on the table, causing silverware to fly over.

"That nigga Gates told you, didn't he? About the woman?"

"Does it matter who told me?" she yelled losing all cool.

As he looked at his beautiful wife, he was taken aback by her jealousy. Finally, he saw the love in her eyes for him. In the past, she made him believe she didn't care but now it was obvious she did. "I don't want to talk about it, Nine."

She leaned in. "What do you mean you don't want to talk about it? You are my husband and I am asking you a question that may affect our marriage. Who is she?"

"When I feel the time is right, I'll let you know." He picked up his fork. "Now, there is nothing more important to me than your sanity. Please eat."

Her right temple pulsated as if someone were tapping repeatedly on it. The anger she felt was blinding, temporarily causing a white cloudy substance to shroud her eyesight. They were tears. "You are my husband—"

"I am," he said cutting her off.

"And yet you believe that it is okay to see another woman and not tell me about it?"

He shook his head. "What I find amazing is that you have maintained a relationship with Gates, the man who lost two daughters on our watch, and I was forced to accept it."

"You never told me not to be friends with him."

"Because I wanted it to be your decision. Not mine."

"And I did cut him off."

"Not before things got out of hand!" He frowned, banging a fist so tight on the table it looked as if his fingers had meshed together and become one. "Not before he fell in love with you!" He paused. "Now, I'll tell you who she is but it will be on my time!"

She stood up, grabbed a napkin off the table and wiped her mouth although she didn't eat a morsel. When she was done she threw it in his face. "I want you out of the mansion tonight."

He was about to lay hands on her but held back. "You can't throw me out of my own home."

She moved away from him and her soldiers blocked his path when he tried to follow. "You are mistaken, cousin. I can prevent you from doing whatever I want and I will."

****

Leaf held Julius in his arms as he walked up to a large multimillion-dollar Georgian-style home. It belonged to his parents whom he hadn't seen in well over a year.

His father Justin and mother Corrine Lincoln were real estate moguls and owned half of the buildings in Baltimore City. It was whispered that the real estate company was nothing more than a drug front for a cartel out of Mexico. But it couldn't be proven and those who kept talking about it found themselves breathing in dirt.

Before knocking on the door, Leaf took another look at the home he grew up in. He recalled some happy memories of playing softball with his father and the huge cookouts with neighbors and friends that his mother hosted. But in his heart he knew something was missing. Never in his life had he dreamed of it being his Prophet heritage.

Leaf took a deep breath and before he could knock, a beautiful forty-something-year-old white woman appeared. She looked different from the last time he saw her. Time had not been kind.

It was Corrine, his mother.

She was shocked, her body trembling, as she observed her only son standing on the other side.

Pushing the screen door open, she took a moment to eye him in silence, each basking in love that was unique to a mother and son. "Autumn," she whispered. "My son."

Unable to hold back any longer, she pulled him into her frail body with the baby between them. At the moment, the child was not a factor in their embrace until he began to cry, demanding attention of his own. Slowly Corrine peeled herself away from Leaf and with tear streaked cheeks, her face dressed with a smile, she asked, "Who is this, Autumn?"

"My son," he said intently.

Corrine placed her fingertips over her quavering lips, looked into Leaf's eyes and then back at the child. "Oh, Autumn…what have you…"

The ending of her sentence disappeared into the ether, for fear she would say the wrong thing and send him away for another year. But the look in her eyes and the way her body stiffened said it all. She did not approve of her son having a child with his cousin and yet she felt as if there was nothing she could do.

If it were true, in her mind, the damage was already done.

"Come in, Autumn. Come inside of your home."

****

With Julius asleep in another room, Leaf sat on the sofa and enjoyed a small lunch of tuna, homemade chips with garlic salt and a glass of wine with his mother. They talked about the neighbors and his family on Corrine's side.

They purposely avoided talk of Prophet business, knowing that there would be plenty of time for that when Justin arrived. And as if on cue, after twenty minutes in relative peace, he busted into the house.

Tossing down his briefcase on the end table, he rushed up to Leaf as if he had no love for him. "What are you doing in my house?"

Despite the anger of his words and the tenseness of his body, Leaf could somehow sense the immense adoration. "I came to see you, Dad." He smiled slightly, hoping to calm him down like he had so many times when they were close. "You and ma. Aren't you happy I'm here? Because I'm happy to see you."

"Justin, please let him alone," Corrine whispered lending as much help as she could. "He just got—"

"I told this boy when he decided to take up with the Prophets that he would no longer be my son." His breaths were so heavy they rocked his core. "I told him that I would disown any child who slept with his own kind under the guise of lust. And yet he left anyway and shared her bed! It's an abomination!"

"I love her, dad," Leaf said calmly. "Is it my fault that you allowed that to happen? Because nobody told me Kerrick was my grandfather. Or that Nine was my cousin." He paused. "Why didn't you tell me about your side of the family? Why didn't you tell me they existed? This is as much your fault as it is mine!"

"I didn't introduce you to them because I don't respect my father's beliefs and I didn't want you exposed to that lifestyle, Autumn! I wanted you to have a chance at a real life with Corrine's family."

"But the Prophets are my family too! I didn't want it to be true but it is!" he yelled placing his hand over his heart. "And it was not your job to keep them away from me!"

When Justin saw his son's tear, he was shocked because he never saw that side of him before. Suddenly Leaf expressed his emotions. Were the Prophets responsible for the change in his son?

"Sleeping with your own kind is not right. And I will never be able to respect that."

Leaf's head dropped. "I love you, dad. I love mom too," he said looking into her eyes before focusing back on Justin.

"But if you push me away, I won't come back." He paused. "Ever. Is that what you want?"

Corrine stood up and walked toward her husband.

"Justin, please. Don't do this to him. Don't do this to me." She paused. "You've been wondering what has happened to me over the past year. Why I've been sick and suddenly developed cancer. I believe it is because I missed my boy." She paused. "Actually, I know it is because I missed him but I was too afraid to feel in front of you, because of how you treat my feelings on the matter. You can act as if he doesn't exist. But I can't. I miss our child. Don't you?"

Upon hearing that his mother had cancer, Leaf stood up and moved toward her slowly, as if he were a zombie. "Mama, you have...you have..." The words were too heavy to utter and yet he needed to know.

"Yes, son. I'm dying. And I prayed for you to come home so that I could see you again. And my prayers have been answered."

With the news confirmed, Leaf stumbled backward and his father caught him before he fell.

CHAPTER SEVENTEEN

"It is not in the stars to hold our destiny but in ourselves."
- William Shakespeare

Naked, Nine twisted the knob leading into her dark private room in search of solitude. It had been days since she'd seen or heard from Leaf and she didn't know quite how she felt. How she was supposed to feel because she had learned to hide her emotions for so long.

The moment her toes pressed against the cool hardwood floor, she knew she was not alone. Was she going crazy again? Defenseless, she asked, "Who is in here?"

"Isabel."

Upon hearing her voice, Nine's tensed body relaxed as she closed the door behind her, darkening the room even more. Although she couldn't see her cousin, she moved toward her energy.

Easing next to her, she leaned her back against the wall and exhaled. "Could not sleep either?" Nine asked.

"Actually it's the opposite. I'm exhausted."

"So why will you not allow yourself to rest?"

"For the first time in my life, I feel at peace and that scares me. More than the colors or even the voices. This place, around you, feels like home."

Nine smiled within the darkness. "Oh, cousin. You and I are more alike than we are different. You can sleep here. It is okay for you to feel at home because you are. Nobody is going to throw you out. Here is where you belong now."

"Why do you think I'm so peaceful?"

"Everything about this home that grandfather built from the ground up has a piece of his thought process inside of it. By being here, maybe unconsciously you feel connected to why he did the things he did, instead of outside of it like a pawn. Grandfather and grandmother lived here and they died here too. Their spirits haunt the walls, I am certain." Nine sighed. "It is the only place on earth where heaven and hell meet in peace."

Isabel nodded in agreement.

"He kept you here, didn't he?" Isabel asked as she looked out ahead into the inky darkness. "Inside this room."

"Yes." She sighed. "And although it was the saddest period of my life, I learned so much by being here. I learned so much by being in solitude. Sometimes when I am out there, in the world, I feel as if I am a stranger. As if I do not belong. The voices, the faces, the motives...all noise."

"The great Nine Prophet feels alone?" Isabel giggled.

"I know...it makes no sense. I command an army of men and yet sometimes, I do not feel qualified. I feel like the girl in this room who no one paid attention to. Who no one knew existed." She paused. "I do not know why I tell you this because I have not ever revealed this much to anyone else, not even my husband."

"You did well by landing him."

"Who?"

"Leaf," Isabel giggled. "Is there anyone else? I can tell he really cares about you."

"And yet he cheats anyway."

"Not sure if a man should be charged for that type of behavior or not. After all things, he is a Prophet and all Prophet men feel the need to have more." She paused. "Still, there's something about him that tells me that he loves only you. Like I said, you lucked up with him. My sisters fight over Noel as if he is the last man standing and I don't think he'll do either of them any good. Besides, he's into men."

Nine exhaled harshly upon hearing the shocking news. "What?" Nine yelled. "How do you know?"

"I've always known. Every male friendship he had ended abruptly. Men don't end relationships abruptly unless they are in love."

"Does Bethany know?"

"Nobody knows but me. I told him I would keep his secret."

"But you did not."

"Telling you does protect his secret, Nine. You are the protector of everybody's secrets. Even mine. Don't you know?"

Nine shook her head in confusion. She never imagined Noel was gay. "Well, at least they will have one child. With Bethany being pregnant now and all."

"That's true," Isabel agreed. "A Prophet is still a Prophet, no matter the parents or their sexuality." She paused. "Nine, I hate to return to Leaf but I still must ask, where is your husband?"

"I put him out."

Silence.

"So you discover he has another woman and then you give him to her?"

"I did not give him to her," Nine said as she stood up and paced the dark room. She didn't allow furniture in the place because of that reason alone. She wanted to move within the shadows without fear of bumping into anything but her thoughts. "Of course I want him to come back to me where he belongs. On his own accord. But I am not about to fight over a woman who in my opinion is not better than I!"

"But you're letting him get away."

"Isabel, your youth has been exposed!" Nine yelled angrily.

"But I'm older than you."

"It is of no consequence! This is real life and you do not fight for men. They fight for you. If he wants me, he has to earn me on hands and knees!" She punched her fist into the palm of her hand. "It is the only way!" Her voice rumbled throughout the room.

"It's trouble," Isabel whispered.

Silence.

Nine walked back over to her cousin and sat against the wall. "Another reason I come here is to be close to my mother, whose blood I did not share." She swallowed, needing to skip the subject about Leaf.

"The one you are naming the wine after?" Isabel questioned. "The maid my mother spoke of?"

"Yes. Grandfather acted as if he did not love her and yet he would not give her body or her heart a pardon to be with another. She fought all of her young life to have him until finally, as an old woman, she realized she would never have him in the way she wanted. When youth was no longer on her side. So she stayed here, imprisoned by her adoration for grandfather, while pouring all of her love into me.

"I will never forget what she told me after she read me a verse from *Romeo and Juliet* one night," Nine continued. "She said, *'Your only concern should be figuring out what a person wants from you and then using that power against them. Love is not worth your life, Nine. Or your time. Always remember that. Take it from me, I know.'*" Nine looked out into the darkness. "And you know what, Isabel, she was right. Because at this moment, my heart burns that there is the slightest possibility that Autumn 'Leaf' Lincoln could not love me as much as I do him. That he could share his body with another woman when he knows the type of violence I am capable of. I do not want my youth to pass me when I could have gotten away from him." She shook her head briskly from left to right. "No, Isabel, I will not fight for any man, even one I love more than I do myself."

Isabel sighed and leaned back into the cool wall. She looked toward the ceiling after taking in everything her cousin said. "Had any crazy episodes lately?"

Nine blinked a few times. "I have."

"Think about what's changed in your life. Think clearly and you'll be able to determine what's off." Isabel stood up and moved toward the door. "You may want to start with your assistant. She's untrustworthy and yet I think you already know that."

Nine laughed. "I do know now." She paused. "People think I am naive and I must admit, at first I was. But it never takes me long to see things in the correct light. Everything clarifies itself for me in time."

Isabel was confused but appreciated Nine's strength.

In a low whisper, Isabel said, "I don't think you're like me. Yet you spend time with me and treat me like we're equals. And that makes you my hero." She moved toward the door and walked out.

****

Nine sat inside of the bank with Mox and Riley, waiting on the banker to return with the key for the safety deposit box. It was payout time for her soldiers, and she was preparing to remove the cash and take it to the academy. The only men she trusted to go with her were the ones who were employed by her grandfather.

After about fifteen minutes, a slender white woman with a pointed nose that bubbled on the tip with pimples walked inside. Her hands remained clasped in front of her and her disposition was rigid. It appeared as if she was trying to be professional but she was coming off as rude. "I'm sorry but we won't be able to give you access."

Nine smiled at first, believing that she was joking. Not only was the money hers, half left to her by her grandfather and the other half earned from making a few smart business investments, everything she owned was in that bank and within the safety deposit boxes.

With her coolness intact, Nine stood up and said, "If this is a joke, I need you to tell me the punch line now." She paused. "Or things are going to get very painful for you."

The woman looked into Nine's eyes and the attitude she possessed suddenly evaporated. She could feel how saying the wrong thing could make a business matter personal and she could end up hurt.

"Ma'am, I'm not telling you a joke. The courts have seized your safety deposit boxes and bank accounts. You should've received notification via mail and by phone." She paused. "Have you?"

****

Nine sat in the back of her Maybach looking at the men assembling for payday at the academy. Security was heightened and the men wore smiles on their faces as they fell into the building. "What am I going to do?" she asked with her gaze fixed upon her soldiers outside of the car. "I have let them down and they will leave me. While I am at war with the Russians."

Mox sighed. "You haven't let them down, Nine. We can still win the fight; it's just that things will have to be done legally."

Slowly her head rotated to where he and Riley sat. Her eyes fell upon theirs. "If I cannot pay them, I have let them down."

Riley looked at her. "Do you know what is happening? With the funds?"

"I have my suspicions," she said filling her lungs with air, before releasing it slowly as she focused on her men again. "The worst part is that I have no idea when this will be settled. I contacted my attorney and he's asking for a retainer to even begin the investigation."

"As much money as you've given him," Mox said. "Shameless."

"Exactly."

"So you keep everything in the bank?" Riley asked. "You don't have any funds outside of it?"

Nine sighed, realizing his question to be an intelligent one. "I never wanted to enter the drug game. I only wanted to run an empire, whatever that might mean. For the Crumbles family, it's real estate, for the Martins, it's casinos and for the Prophets, it's cocaine." She paused. "I understood my position when I took over the responsibility. *Fully*. Still, my objective was to make sure that no family member with a Prophet name would go without. Ever. So that even if I died, money would still remain in this family for generations to come. And that required legalizing the business. So I placed everything in the legal ventures, so that the government would never be able to take anything away from us. But, I underestimated the power of my family's capacity for greed."

Silence.

"You asked if I have any other money available…the answer is no," she continued.

"Nine, go home. We'll tell the men what is going on," Mox said.

"I would never put that dishonor on you two," she said calmly. "You do not deserve it and I fight my own battles."

Mox got up and sat next to her. He placed his hand on hers, which rested on her thigh. "Your grandfather once told me that you would make a fair leader and at the time I didn't understand what he meant. Because you were so young. You're still young now. But, I finally understand." He paused. "Go before your men with a pure heart and although it may not seem like it in the moment, they will receive you, even if it's later."

Nine wanted to believe him but she knew that men desired money and when she did not make it available, they could attack. And yet she had no other choice but to deal with the matter head on.

****

Nine looked upon the sea of men, all assembled and waiting for her. On payout days, she would often start with a thank you for their service, hand out the payouts and then a meal. It felt more like a corporation than a drug operation. But the moment she parted her lips to speak and closed them again, every man present knew something was wrong. She was usually poised.

Realizing that bad news or not, she had to deliver, she looked down at her hands, which flopped on the podium. "There will not be a payout today."

The room temperature went up one degree due to the exhalation of the breath and the anger inside of the room. The reason for the tension was simple. Working for Nine Prophet and the Prophet family was only one aspect of their lives. Most of the men had families and children to care for.

What were they to do now?

Although originally everyone disputed the payout being done only twice a year, each man believed in her and was always rewarded handsomely for waiting and it reflected in the amount given. They were always given extra. They had even gotten used to the long time frame and learned to balance their money accordingly. But never, ever, had any soldier present considered not getting paid.

Business was good.

They all knew it, so what was happening?

It was her youth that had been exposed.

When he sensed her distraught behavior, Antonius rose from his seat to console her. But she motioned for him to remain where he was, fearing his men would not respect him if he rushed to the side of the woman who hurt them all. His position was next to his men where it belonged.

"A family matter that I did not see coming has put a hold on business and I am so sorry. Had I predicted this could have happened, I would have prepared for it in advance. I do not know how but I will make this right. I just need a little more time."

"But what about our families?" yelled a man in the back. "We have bills too!"

"I know," she said humbly. "Which is why this is the toughest thing I have ever had to do in my life."

"We know you have some money tucked away somewhere," yelled another. "You sell dope! So what about cracking that stash and giving us our paper?" he screamed. "I bet you still eating!"

"Foolishly, I placed all that I have, every dime, away where I thought it would be safe. If I had anything left, I would give it to you gladly."

One by one, men she thought loved her got up and expressed their displeasure with wild arms and distorted faces. Her heart ached as she saw the disappointment in their eyes while knowing they had a right to their pain. She messed up royally and the only thing they wanted was for her to make things right.

But where would she start?

****

Nine stood at the window looking at the vineyard. It had been a week since she held her meeting with the soldiers and out of frustration, she threw herself into solitude, speaking to no one. Not her husband. Not her assistant or the Nobles.

She wanted to be alone, in the hopes that some idea would emerge in her mind to clear her financial troubles. And so far, nothing presented itself.

She allowed Isabel to remain in the mansion, within her space, because it was almost as if she wasn't there. Not unlike Nine, Isabel got lost in the walls of the house and for days, they would not see or talk to one another.

She was a perfect roommate.

Although she was still at a loss for words, Nine noticed that the crazy visions disappeared. She was grateful for that. At least her thoughts would be clear, not even tainted with alcohol.

Leaf called for the first few days to reconnect but after Nine ignored him each time, he stopped. In the end, she pulled the phone out of the wall and sat her cell phone in a pot of boiling water so that she could be left alone.

As Nine continued to gaze outside, she marveled at how things seemed different. Since her soldiers were not paid, there was no one guarding her or the property. If someone were smart, it would be an opportune time to attack. But it was as if even her enemies felt as if she wasn't worth their time.

Spending moments alone allowed her to contemplate a lot of things. The fact that her family, with Alice in the lead, had taken away her ability to care for herself and others.

She should have killed her when she had the time. She thought about murdering her now. But it was too late. If she showed up dead, the courts would suspect her immediately.

Nine was still waiting on word from the lawyer she tried to attain, to see if he would take the case and be paid if they won as opposed to up front. But as of now, he had yet to respond.

She also wondered how Julius was doing and if Leaf's new woman was replacing her. She was falling deeper into depression until there was a soft knock at the front door. Nine strolled toward the sound, wondering who could be visiting. The request to the world to leave her alone had obviously gone ignored.

When she opened the door, a strange woman she didn't recognize greeted her. Her white face was extremely wrinkled and the whites of her eyes were yellowish, giving her a sinister appeal. The two-piece blue suit she wore was loaded with lint balls and she donned a white pair of sweat socks in a pair of beaten down old blue leather high heels. The two thin lines that were her lips were smeared with lipstick too red for her pale skin.

"Ah, ain't you a beautiful sight," the woman said clutching a black leather bible with assorted Post-It tabs hanging from the edge of the pages. "Just a cute little nigger child."

Nine stepped forward about to snatch her throat out. "What did you call me?"

"A cute little child," she smiled, making Nine believe she was going crazy again. "I must admit, TV doesn't do you any justice."

Nine clutched her pink robe closed and when she gazed to her right, Isabel was standing beside her. And for some reason, Nine was relieved.

"Who are you?" Nine asked coldly.

"My name is Sister Anna Marie Cartwright but you can call me mama."

Isabel frowned. "Why would she call you mama? You ain't related." She didn't like the woman one bit although she just met her.

"I don't believe I've had the pleasure of knowing you," Anna said, with bits of hostility in her voice. "What's your name?"

"Answer her question," Nine interrupted.

Anna readjusted and said, "You don't have to call me mama if you don't want to. It's just that all of the children I've ever cared for in my life have. It's more of an endearing moniker than anything else."

"Why are you at my home?" Nine persisted.

Anna readjusted her stance and gripped her bible tighter. "I'm here on a matter which is far from personal," she smiled. "I run a homeless shelter for children and unfortunately we aren't government funded. I was hoping that you could—"

"Wait a minute," Nine recollected. "You called me some weeks back. And said that something happened with one of my family members." She paused. "You also said that if I handled things properly, you could make the matter go away." Nine lowered her eyes. "Who are you and what do you *really* want?"

Anna's mood suddenly changed. "Okay, I'll shoot straight from my boots." She cleared her throat. "I'm afraid your uncle Joshua has found himself in an impossible position. Now normally I can perform miracles, seeing as how I'm ordained and all."

Nine and Isabel looked at each other and back at her again.

"But even this matter is beyond my power," Anna continued.

"And what is the situation?" Nine asked.

"He's in charge of a shelter for children and there is one little girl he's quite fond of. And although he hasn't touched her yet, I can see that it's possible in his eyes, Mrs. Prophet. Now I don't have to tell you why I'm worried. It's been all over the news, about Bethany and Samantha."

"What the fuck is that supposed to mean?" Isabel yelled hearing her sisters' names.

"It's just that the Prophet lineage makes you susceptible to vile acts of nature. You do participate in incest, correct? Because rape is the next thing. I don't mean any disrespect, but I'm afraid he'll have his way with this child soon enough if someone doesn't intervene."

By T. Styles   163

"So just stop him from being around her," Isabel advised, realizing if he hadn't done anything yet, the troubles would be over.

Anna's emotions changed three times upon hearing Isabel's voice. She went from fake concern for the child at the shelter, to anger for Isabel butting in on her business, to an old woman exhibiting helpless behavior. "Who am I to stop it? I'm just a worn out old woman who hasn't got two cents to rub together for sparks. I can't stop a grown man from doing anything he pleases," she assured them. "It's outside of my hands unless...well...unless."

"Spit it out," Nine yelled.

"Well unless you give us some money to build our new wing. Perhaps I can also use a portion of the funds to bring in some able-bodied men to protect the children once and for all. You have millions, I'm only asking for a few hundred thou."

"He is not even a Prophet," Nine explained. "His last name is Saint."

"Do you think people will be concerned about him or your aunt Marina? Who *is* a Prophet." She paused. "Last name or not, he's still in the family and all family behavior leads back to you."

Nine trembled with anger. It was clear that she was there to blackmail her and Nine didn't have respect for snakes. "Never come here again," she warned. "Never come here for money or news of my family. Am I clear?"

"Did you hear me, child?" she yelled. "If this matter is not resolved, it could get out of hand and cause major problems for you and your family. Think of the peace if you don't think of the children!"

"It is not my problem!" Nine slammed the door in her face.

Isabel looked over at Nine and said, "She's going to be the reason that life for the Prophets, as we know it, will change. Forever."

"I know, Isabel," Nine sighed. "I know."

****

Nine was lying in bed when Isabel opened the bedroom door excitedly with an iPad in her hand. "Look at this," she said as she crawled on top of the bed and leaned against the headboard.

Nine removed the iPad from her fingers and scanned it briefly. She gazed over at her and said, "What am I looking for?"

"This is the woman who came by earlier," she said pointing at her strange face on the screen. "She has a history of blackmailing people for money to avoid scandal."

Nine sat up in the bed, leaned against the headboard and reviewed the articles slowly.

'Sister Anna Marie Cartwright takes on Pope in altar boy case'. *'Sister Anna Marie Cartwright protests against married New York senator and his alleged gay lover'.*

On and on the articles spoke about how Anna got involved in matters that didn't concern her. And although a few of them reported being blackmailed, no one bothered to follow up on the charges because of the nature of the cases. In the end, the scandal would always die down and Nine couldn't help but wonder if the headlines died because Anna was being paid to go away quietly.

Frustrated, Nine tossed the iPad down.

"You think she'll do something like this to us?"

Nine closed her eyes and reopened them slowly. "Call Joshua and—"

"I'm not talking to him," Isabel snapped. "I fucking hate that man!"

"He is your uncle." She paused. "Do it for me, Izzy. Call him and tell him that whatever girl he is hanging around, for his own good, he had better stop." She paused. "Tell him about this woman and her plans to expose him in the media. Remind him that being labeled a pedophile is a brand that never shakes. Even if he is found not guilty."

"You think that will stop her?"

"I am hoping so, although I probably should not care. Outside of him, she has nothing on us. With time, this will more than likely go away. But I do know this...I will never give her a dime. Ever."

CHAPTER EIGHTEEN

"There is nothing either good or bad, but thinking makes it
so."
-William Shakespeare

Bottles of half-empty liquor lay around Victory's house as Alice danced around the living room looking at her family who were sitting somberly on the couch.

She was in celebration mode and, in her selfishness, could care less how they felt.

Although no one was as happy as she was about having the Prophet accounts frozen, she was determined not to let them steal her joy. When she started singing, Noel, Victory, Marina and Blake looked up at her as if she was a foolish child behaving badly and at the moment, she was.

"You know this is a mistake, right?" Noel said, already wrecked with guilt for betraying Nine. "You putting a hold on the money means that Nine couldn't pay her men. You should've seen the look on her face when she had to walk out of that building after telling them she didn't have it. She couldn't even pay my father and me. Now we all have to wait pending the court trial."

Alice stopped dancing. "Oh, Noel, why do you whine so much? You're so busy worried about a few bucks when if all goes well, you'll have millions." She paused. "Why do you care who she pays and when?"

"Because I saw her face when she had to face the men," Noel pleaded. "Her heart was broken, Alice. I knew in that moment that although she desires power, Nine sincerely wants the best for everybody." He looked at his parents and uncle. "Even us."

Alice stared down at him. Her chest grew swollen with hot air every time she breathed in. "You are sitting over there so self-righteous when it was you who brought us the video of her acting out at her house." She laughed. "You went over there like you were a friend to Leaf and the whole time you were snapping videos of her trying to crawl out the window. Cousin, without you, there would not have been a case!"

"I know what I did," he said with a lowered head and heavy heart. "And that's the part that makes me feel the worst."

"You shouldn't feel worse," Alice continued. "You shouldn't feel anything. I mean, do you honestly believe that it's right that she be able to dictate our lot in life?"

"She's right, son," Victory said softly. "For reasons I'll never know, Nine has been given domain over our family and it should not be that way."

"She doesn't have domain over us!" Noel yelled.

"Son, she who holds the money rules," Blake said.

"And that means she's in charge," Alice said slyly. "And before I stepped in, she had it all. The only thing we have to do as a group is stick together and vote to have her pushed out. That's it."

Noel looked up into her eyes. "You just want to drag us all to hell for company. You know in your heart that your days are numbered for whatever you did to her. You know you're operating on borrowed time." He paused. "It wasn't enough for you to go alone. You had to take everybody with a Prophet name down with you."

Alice stood in the middle of the floor trembling with anger. She tightened her fists and imagined using them on his temples. "If you don't want the money, don't take it, Noel. The last thing I want to do is push you."

Silence.

She walked over to where he sat and grabbed her purse that sat on the floor next to him. She removed a pad and a pen, tossed her bag on the floor and handed them to him. "As a matter of fact, sign a note indicating that you don't want any of the fortune when this is all said and done. And I promise you won't get a cent."

Noel looked down at the journal, opened the book and rubbed the first cool page. As if he was about to write something, the tip of the pen hovered over the empty blue line. Suddenly the pen was too heavy between his fingers and it toppled to the floor.

He gazed up at Alice and she grinned.

"She's going to kill us," he whispered. He looked at his family. "She's going to kill every last one of us."

Alice giggled. "Then let there be blood."

****

Banker pulled up in front of the Prophet Mansion and parked in her normal spot. It had been weeks since she'd been to work and surprisingly she couldn't wait to return. Besides, it was almost time for her trip to Aruba and she needed to write one more check from Nine's account before she left.

Originally, she was supposed to go with Galileo but when he told her he didn't have any money, because Nine held back on the payouts, she cut him off. She tried to make amends but he never returned her calls.

She learned her greed honestly. As the daughter of a rich man who cut back on paying her expenses, because she dropped out of school after her sister was murdered, she was used to being given anything she desired. And when she started dating Galileo, she expected him to supply her every greedy need.

He failed but she realized she loved him anyway.

When she opened the front door and walked toward the dining room where Nine preferred to do business, Banker was shocked when she saw her boyfriend sitting at the table. He wore a wide smile and at first that put her at ease.

Maybe he and Nine squashed their differences.

Maybe she didn't know they were together.

Maybe everything was cool.

Maybe she was just tripping.

Gracefully, Nine stood up and the elegant royal blue gown she wore dusted her ankles. "Come over here, Banker." She smiled widely. "And have a seat."

With a grin on her face, due to the excitement about seeing her boyfriend, she moved toward them. Once there, she sat down at the table and said, "Sorry I'm late, Nine. I got here as fast as I could."

"I know you did," Nine nodded. "We are about to have a meal and I wanted you to join us. So actually, you are just in time. But before doing that, let us have a drink." She paused and looked back toward the kitchen. "Isabel, please bring me the bottle of wine from the cooler."

Banker's face drooped like a snowman that had been in the sun too long.

"It's okay," Banker said knowing that she had poisoned all of the wine in the house with a little Phenethylamine, a drug more potent than acid. "I don't want anything."

Although she only gave Nine trace amounts, just enough to destroy her facilities, delirium was one of the side effects of the poison. And was Alice's plan to get her off the throne.

However, the bottle of the evening had a little something extra inside, courtesy of Nine.

"Well I do," Galileo responded as he rubbed his hands together. Although he knew his girlfriend had some beef with the boss, he had no idea about her methods of destruction. As a matter of fact, he had limited knowledge about her period.

Isabel poured Galileo a glass of wine and watched him wash it down, before tossing back another.

"G, slow down," Banker said, wanting him to stop all together. "It's not that deep."

"But it's good shit, baby," he responded sipping some more.

Despite four people being present, there were only two glasses on the table. Not wanting Galileo to drink alone, Isabel walked toward Banker and put a glass in front of her. Then she moved back behind Nine and placed a warm hand on her shoulder. Both of them observed Banker who had tears crawling out of her eyes.

She was caught and was out of her league.

"When we are born, we cry that we are come to this great stage of fools," Nine said quoting Shakespeare. "Do you know what that means, Banker?"

Banker shook her head no.

"Drink the wine and I will tell you more."

When Galileo finally realized that his girlfriend was having a quiet battle with Nine and Isabel, he became concerned. What really was going on? Why was he there? He positioned his body so that he could face Nine. He felt powerful against her, seeing as though not one of the soldiers of the Legion was present. "Hold up," he huffed, "what's going on here?" Suddenly he started to feel crazy and kept closing and opening his eyes to clear his vision.

"What is going on is that you have a .45 caliber handgun pointed at your nuts under the table," Nine said. "You are a shoddy shot, Gene," she looked into his eyes, "but I am not. Now turn around and put your hands on the table before I smack the shit out of you first."

Fearful of becoming a woman by a horrible surgery, he remained still. But why did he feel loopy?

Focusing back on Banker, Nine said, "Drink...the...wine."

"Yeah, bitch, taste your own blood," Isabel said sneering at her. She knew something was up with her the moment she laid eyes on her. And when Nine had Dr. Banning test the wine and it came up poisonous, she felt validated.

There were some other things Nine learned about Banker too but those things would be revealed later. And she told no one. Not even Isabel.

With a shaky hand, Banker reached across the table and took the wine. The edge of the glass rested against her bottom lip and a few tears splashed inside of the glass. Hoping Nine would recant her request, she tilted the glass up and the wine rolled down slowly like thick honey crawling toward the spout of a half empty jar. Nine's eyes remained on her, while the gun nestled in her hand was still aimed at Galileo who felt loopier than ever.

The drug was affecting him.

When she was finished, Nine leaned back and decided to humor her before the poison took hold. "The statement I made was by Shakespeare," Nine said as if Banker cared. "He is my favorite author." She looked over at Galileo and then Banker. "The passage, *'When we are born, we cry that we are come to this great stage of fools,'* means many things for different people. But I believe it means that babies cry when they enter this world because they are amongst fools. Like I have been recently, with you and Gene. But the difference between them and me is that in a little while, I will not be."

"I knew you were a snake," Isabel said. "It was all in your eyes."

"Tell me, Banker," Nine interjected. "What did Alice give you to poison my wine a little at a time?"

She swallowed. "Phenethylamine."

"But why not just kill her?" Isabel asked.

"I know why," Nine winked. "It took me some time but I finally found out."

Galileo's shoulders tightened. "Can somebody please tell me what the fuck is going on? And what did I drink? I feel fucking crazy!" Galileo yelled. Balls of sweat developed from his hairline and trickled down the sides of his face.

Nine positioned her body so that she could clearly see into his eyes. With a slow disbelieving headshake, she said, "You are the worst kind of man. You took away a good mother from your child, all because you did not want to pay support!" Her fist came down on the table so hard it cracked slightly under her blow. "What kind of bum are you?"

"I didn't do anything," he lied trying to remain sane although the drugs were really working on him. "I...I...she was killed by somebody else."

"Sure she was," Nine said firing into his groin. She was tired of looking at him and he was worth no more of her time. When she was finished, she raised the gun and fired into the center of his forehead.

Suddenly Isabel's posture stiffened. Looking upon the bloody mess at the table, she said, "I guess what I heard about you was true. You are violent."

"There is an ounce of truth to every rumor. But be careful what you believe."

Isabel squeezed her eyes shut and opened them again. She was horrified and exhilarated at the same time. "Well, this has been quite an event, hasn't it?" She looked over at Banker and then down at Nine. "So what are we going to do with her?"

"I have a plan. We are just getting started."

CHAPTER NINETEEN

"Hell is empty and all the devils are here."
- William Shakespeare

Nine lay in the bed until she heard someone enter her home. Although she was upstairs, many square feet away from the front door, it was eerily quiet and she could hear it all. Every floor creak. Every swoosh of air rushing past the windowpane and most of all, intruders. After taking care of Banker and Galileo, she required much sleep and now it had been broken.

Upon hearing the noise, Isabel, who was sleeping in the bed next to her, popped up. "You heard it too?" Isabel asked rubbing her eyes before yawning.

Nine eased out of bed. "Heard is past tense. I'm still hearing it." She was about to move toward the door when it opened and the light flipped on. Suddenly she was staring into the eyes of her husband. In his arms, he was clutching Julius, who was draped in a warm red North Face coat and new Jordans.

The moment she saw their faces, all of the anxiety she had experienced was removed. Although coolness became her, she was now trembling, realizing in that moment that she was blithe to see him. Without a word to his wife, he laid Julius down in the crib and removed his coat, tossing it on the chair across the room. When he was done he took off his black jacket also.

Before moving to Nine, Leaf looked over at Isabel and then back at his wife and said, "So I guess one cousin isn't good enough for you."

"Do not be rude, Leaf," Nine said as she sat on the edge of the bed and looked up at him. "At first I was happy to see you but do not make me change my mind."

He sat next to her. "We have to talk." He looked back at Isabel. "Alone."

"I'm gone," she said as she hopped out of the bed. "Welcome back, Leaf. Glad to have you home." She ran toward the door and out of the bedroom.

He looked over at Nine again.

"Prophets are everywhere these days."

"It is not like that, Leaf. So get that noise out of your head."

He smiled. "I'm just kidding."

Nine sighed, looked down at her fingers and back at him. "I need to know who she is, Leaf. You never gave me the benefit of an answer and I need to know now. Instead, you treated me like—"

"I haven't treated you like anything, bae! You're the one who's been disrespecting me. I don't need your fucking money, Nine. I come from dough! I'm in this marriage, as fucked up as it is, because I love you. But if you can't love me back…"

"All I want to do is love you, cousin. That is all I ever wanted to do." She paused. "Where were you?"

"I went to see my parents," he responded in a low voice. "My mother is dying of cancer and…"

"I am so sorry, cousin," Nine said compassionately. "Is there anything I can—"

"I don't want to talk about it. Not right now anyway." At the moment, for the sake of Corrine, he and his father were on speaking terms but the relationship was far from repaired. But no matter what, he would not keep him from his mother.

She nodded in understanding. "How is Julius?" she asked looking over at him sleeping in the crib. "Do you think he misses me?"

"I know that he does. At first he would not cry when he saw my face but when I tried to pick him up after a few days, he wouldn't stop hollering. My mother couldn't even calm him and she's cool with kids."

"You know when I heard that noise, I thought you were somebody breaking in. So much has happened since you left, Leaf. I do not have any money and all of the men who are usually here left and I am unprotected."

By T. Styles   175

Leaf felt bad although he was right. He predicted this moment. The moment she lost the money, her men would abandon her. "As long as I'm here, you'll never be unprotected."

"Then do not go away again," she said holding his hand.

He winked at her.

"Wait a minute," he said as if he remembered something. "You didn't make the noise when I was bringing the baby upstairs?" He paused. "That's why I came inside."

Her eyes widened. "No. I mean…I heard something and then you came in."

"Naw, bae. Little man and me been here for at least an hour. I got in late so I was about to chill in one of the other rooms and then I heard something moving inside of the house."

They took a moment to look at one another, realizing the ultimate. Someone without authorization was still in their home. Could it be the Russians? On cue, she grabbed her weapon and he snatched his. But before they could react, the room was flooded with a small army of men, with Antonius leading them. Leaf pushed Nine toward the back of the room and he drew his revolver and aimed in their direction.

Nine's heart beat rapidly because she could not believe Antonius was about to betray her, when out of all of her men she loved him the most.

"Nine, what is going on?" Antonius asked. His voice was full of so much concern that she was suddenly relaxed.

"What do you mean what is going on?" Nine asked. "You busted up in my house!"

Leaf stood in front of his wife, preparing to hit as many niggas as he could with a bullet before they killed them both. "Yeah, fuck you doing in our house, man?" Leaf asked with authority while still aiming. "I would've thought this would be anybody but you."

"I'm here because Nine wouldn't answer the phone."

"So you keep trying," Leaf said. "You don't break in somebody's house."

"But it's been days!" He paused. "And I got tired of waiting…so I…so I…"

"Broke in," Leaf responded, finishing his sentence.

"No, man. It's not like that. We're here to protect her."

"Even if it were true, I still do not have any money to pay you, Antonius," Nine said speaking from the heart. "Or the men."

"You've done more things for us than anybody we ever pumped coke for. You didn't want us to just tote a gun. You taught us the importance of family and honor. Why wouldn't we protect you at a time like this? We reward loyalty with loyalty," Antonius stated quoting what Nine told him the night she found his missing daughter.

Nine wanted to weep but thought it would be considered soft. Still, the loyalty they were displaying was top notch and much unexpected. "How many others feel like you?" Nine asked.

"About thirty of us are here but nine hundred of the original thousand remain loyal." He paused. "Listen, we don't give a fuck about the money. We know we'll get that back when the time is right. The only thing we care about right now is protecting you. And if we have to lay a few niggas down for free to make that happen, then so be it."

Now Leaf was relaxed although confused. He knew Antonius and out of all of the men in Nine's camp, he respected him the most. Finally, he lowered his weapon. "What you mean lay a few niggas down for free?"

Antonius' eyes widened. "Wait, you don't know?"

"Know what?" Nine questioned.

"We got word from the Kennedys that the Russians are sending some niggas over here as we speak to attack. We have to get ready. We at war!"

****

Darkness acted as a cover as the Russians' soldiers appeared on foot, down a road that led to the Prophet Mansion. Arkadi, the leader who had recently lost a brother due to the Kennedy Kings' vengeance, realized that he needed to disable the Kennedy Kings operation like they had his own.

So he aimed for the Kennedys' most powerful ally.

The Prophets.

Slowly, fifty men descended upon the walkway leading closer to the acres of land the Prophet mansion sat on. Confidently, they continued down the way until they reached the gate. One man after the other, with automatic assault rifles in hand, approached.

To their surprise, the iron gate surrounding the land was open at the entrance as if it were beckoning them to come inside. The leader of Arkadi's army, a 45-year-old navy seal, placed a finger over his lips to silence his men and to warn them to move slowly and cautiously. He was listening for the sound that indicated that they were not alone.

Feeling as if the coast was clear, he motioned for them to merge onto the Prophet compound. But the moment the first boot stepped past the gate, bright lights spilled over the land, exposing everything in sight.

"Wait," the leader yelled, raising his fist at his men. The fog would not allow them to see a foot in front of them and he wanted to spare as many men as possible.

When the ex-navy seal saw red dots all over his soldiers' foreheads he knew what was happening, they were in danger. Within seconds, gunfire blasted from the mansion, killing every soldier in sight, except the commander.

With the souls of his dead men in the air, the smell of gunpowder and blood enveloped him, and a cloud of smoke made it even more difficult to see the mansion. Suddenly he heard a calm feminine voice. "Put down your weapon."

"No," he yelled as he aimed into the thick fog. "I'm not letting you kill me!"

The woman giggled. "Look at your jacket, soldier. If I wanted you dead, you'd be gone now."

When he glanced down, he saw his jacket was speckled with red dots as if he were a Christmas tree. Slowly he lowered his weapon and raised his hands. After a few seconds, from behind the smoke came Nine. Dressed in a chocolate fur coat, she moved closer to him.

He didn't know if he was enamored by her beauty or fearful of her quiet power. Either way, she had his attention.

"I am Nine Prophet and I will let you live," she said calmly.

His knees felt weak by the octave of her voice.

"On one condition," she continued.

Trembling as if he never served a day in the military in his life, he said, "Anything."

"You tell your boss that what happened here tonight is only a fraction of the power I possess. You let him know that I can touch his family and anyone else he cares about if he ever comes back here." She paused. "I am a dangerous woman and he should heed my warning."

CHAPTER TWENTY
TWO WEEKS LATER

"We know what we are, but not what we may be."
- William Shakespeare

Alice paced the floor in the conference room of the attorney's office and she was in an unspeakable mood. Victory, Noel, Blake and Marina were sitting around the table waiting on their lawyer who called late last night for an emergency meeting. When asked what the conference was about, they were told he would explain everything later.

"I don't know what the fuck he wants," Alice grumbled as she stopped moving and sat down in her chair next to Noel. Her leg jiggled rapidly.

"Did he say anything else to you?" Victory asked. White cat hair sat on the table in front of her and on her black dress jacket, even though no animal was in sight.

She sighed, her heart thumping wildly in her chest. "No. Just that we all needed to be here. And on time." She paused and stood up again. "Fuck!" she yelled startling them. "And then nobody has seen or heard from Nine in weeks. I just hope she doesn't have anything to do with this."

"Alice, just shut the fuck up," Marina yelled rubbing her arms rapidly. "For five seconds, please! You're making me antsy and I need a hit. Messing with you, I've had to do things to get my medicine I never dreamed. All because I don't have any money. If this doesn't work, I don't know what I'm going to do."

Alice's face turned downward. "I'm sorry, mama. Didn't mean to upset you."

"Don't be sorry! Just don't fuck up!"

Alice twisted the watch on her arm.

"This is not good," Blake said to himself as his gaze darted from the door to the space in front of him. "Not good at all."

When the door finally opened, Brett Jones walked inside and tried to avoid eye contact with the worried family. But Alice was all over his ass the moment he sat down. "What the fuck is going on? We're all here now what?"

Brett sat a manila folder on the table and pushed it to the side, before clasping his hands in front of him. "There's been a problem."

"A problem?" Alice said as she tugged on the collar of her shirt. "How you figure?"

"Yesterday morning Nine was able to meet with the judge and had him lift the freeze on all banking accounts by having the majority Prophet rule. I don't know all the facts yet but somehow she was able to put the case back in her favor."

"Put the case back in her favor?" Alice repeated. "How?"

His legs moved restlessly under his body. "She was also able to prove to the judge that not only was she not crazy, but that she was being poisoned."

Alice's foot bounced around as she thought about everything she'd done up to that point. From the moment she met Banker and gave her the Phenethylamine poison to put in the wine a little at a time, she had been manipulating the situation. She didn't want Nine dead, not yet anyway. If she died, the money would be left to Julius or Leaf. She had to keep her alive and convince the courts that she was not suitable to be at the head of the estate.

Whatever happened to her after that would be an accident.

"Poisoned by who?" Alice asked.

"By you," he responded.

The moment he made the statement, she knew who betrayed her. Her least favorite cousin, Noel. Instead of looking at her, he lowered his head and closed his eyes as if he were praying. "I couldn't do her like that, man," he said softly, gazing at his family. "You didn't tell us you was poisoning her. She's good people; you just have to—"

"Son, why didn't you tell us you was going to do this?" Blake asked. He released the navy blue tie from around his neck and tossed it on the table. "You knew she fired me. I was depending on this money to take care of myself. We could've jumped on board with you!"

"Oh, my God, Noel. What were you thinking?" Victory continued. "How selfish do you have to be to go behind our backs and not even alert us?"

"Because this way he comes out as a hero," Alice responded coldly. "And we look like the bad guys." She paused. "You're a snake! After everything we went through. I was the one who taught you how to fuck. How to make a woman feel good and this is how you repay me? You were nothing without me, Noel! Remember how you begged me to stick my finger in your asshole so you could cum quicker? I don't even think you like girls!"

Although the Prophet family was surprised to find out that Noel and Alice had slept together, it wasn't a big deal in the scheme of everything.

It was Brett Jones who was at a loss for words.

"You said something else," Victory responded trying to take her mind off of her dysfunctional family. "About Nine getting the majority Prophet rule. How is that possible?"

He cleared his throat. "I don't know. Are there any other Prophets with your bloodline?"

"Yes, but I know they wouldn't help her."

"Are you sure?"

"I can't be sure," she said in a defeated tone. She was more upset that she allowed Alice to convince her to get involved with the plight than anything else. "But my brother Justin, her husband's father, is still out there somewhere."

"Yeah but he doesn't respect our side of the family," Marina said as she appeared more fidgety due to going into withdrawals. "I can't see him helping her."

"Me either," Blake responded. "He doesn't have anything to do with our family or Nine so I can't see him getting involved."

"As of now, there are eleven living Prophets," Victory explained. "Five are here (Blake, me, Marina, Noel, Alice) and three more are my daughters. So we have the majority."

"But where are your children?" the lawyer asked.

"Bethany and Samantha are at home on house arrest and Isabel..." Blake looked over at Victory. "Isabel is staying with Nine."

When Victory's phone dinged, she saw it was a text from Bethany. *'Mama, something crazy is on the door. Where are you?'*

She ignored the message.

Brett sat back and looked at all of them. "Well, someone is assisting her. That you don't know about." The expression on his face showed he'd given up on helping them. They were a lost cause.

There was a slight knock at the door and in walked Nine, Leaf, Isabel and four other people whose complexions were lighter than theirs and could be confused for white.

Although Alice and the others didn't know it, they were full-blooded members of the Prophet family.

Always a man of great appetite, many years ago, Kerrick had an affair with Bridget Danker. A beautiful black woman with skin so light she could pass for white. The moment he met her, she was a breath of fresh air. Not because of her beauty but because unlike Victoria and Fran, Bridget was an adventurer.

Through her he was able to pursue the wilder side of life and he found himself at home in her energy, in her presence. Whether it was skydiving or rock climbing, she was a child in a woman's body always looking for a new rush.

And then she got pregnant.

The first child, Lisa, she hid from him by causing a petty argument over him speaking to her harshly about a meal she prepared for dinner one night. The disagreement was foolish and planned because she needed a reason to break ties. Young Kerrick would've snapped her neck for disrespect but Bridget caught him at an older age.

But she wasn't stupid. Kerrick's legend preceded him and she knew that he wasn't a man who dealt easily with children outside of his marriage. She heard stories of Fran whose womb he had destroyed for the same behavior. Still, she was determined not to abort the child so there was a decision to be made. Stay with him and give up her baby or cut things off. Not believing in abortion, she chose the latter. And although she missed him, and he her, she felt resolved in her decision.

Some months later, Kerrick learned that she was pregnant. At first he sent Mox, Riley and Jameson to "get rid of the problem" but when he saw her, he was amazed that even while pregnant Bridget seemed to glow. Going against his rule, he allowed her to live. And he allowed her to carry his child.

He felt validated in allowing her to bear his child when he saw Lisa, and to his surprise, Lisa's beauty rivaled her mother's. As the years passed, Lisa grew into her gorgeousness. Her big stunning eyes and long black luscious hair made her sexually appealing to all men who encountered her. But she was a Prophet, which also meant she was off limits without Kerrick's approval.

After Lisa was born, Kerrick placed money in Bridget's bank account for their wellbeing, to ensure that his child would never have to go without. They didn't have the classic rich Prophet lifestyle but it was a come up.

Things were going good and a year later, she got pregnant with boy triplets and this time she didn't run, she let Kerrick know. Since Bridget handled his marriage so well in the past, never bothering to contact his wife, he allowed her another honor. On one condition. That she explained to them how important it was to keep their bloodline pure.

At first Bridget was disgusted at the idea alone. But Kerrick was a great orator and he explained that his lineage came from the kings and queens of Africa. In his delusion, he talked about how intelligent his older children were and how even in Roman times incest was accepted.

Before long, she was sold and when her children were born she allowed Kerrick to push the same rigid beliefs into their minds. As a result, Lisa had a son by her oldest brother Wagner, who she named Kerrick II.

Kerrick's sex-starved energy made some wonder if there were any other Prophets out there that no one knew about.

As the new Prophets made themselves comfortable in the conference room, Lisa first, followed by the triplets Wagner, Porter and Jeremy, the other Prophets wondered what was happening. Each of them was beautiful and flawed.

For instance, one of Wagner's eyes were cocked, due to wearing a pair of prescription glasses when he didn't need them as a child, just to look like a local street killer in his neighborhood.

And then there was the middle child. Although as handsome as the other male siblings, Porter kept his top lip pulled down because his teeth were crumbled, due to not taking care of them.

Lastly, there was Jeremy, who lost his arm recently when his brothers and sister busted into an abandoned house where his mother was being gang raped. They successfully saved her but they got into a war with the gang that was looking for them at the moment. This was why Lisa, the girl Nine had seen in the photos Gates showed her, attempted to reach out to Nine by way of Leaf.

When Lisa first approached him, he doubted they were related. He was used to people trying to get close to Nine to access her money by claiming to share the bloodline. So he hid the matter from his wife for fear she'd get involved and be taken advantage of.

However, Lisa was persistent and suggested blood tests be taken. She was a Prophet and was willing to prove it. He could tell in her eyes that she wasn't going away so he had the tests performed and was waiting on the results. So when Nine lashed out at him in the restaurant, he was willing to eat the L to make sure he kept fakes away from her because the tests had yet to come in.

Nine and the new Prophets stood on the other side of the table, next to Alice's lawyer. Antonius and five other men stood outside of the door on guard. Upon first entering the office, Nine felt powerful but when she walked in and saw the faces of the family members she'd grown to love, it was as if a pin was stuck into her balloon.

She realized at that moment that she cared for them but the betrayal changed something in her spirit. She was starting to hate them. No longer was she going to be pushed over by those who didn't deserve her love or money. If they wanted to bite the hand that fed them, then they would be on their own.

She looked down at Alice and the others and said, "I do not look like you. I do not dress like you or talk like you. But I am still your blood. I am still a Prophet and it is sad that you could not see it." She sighed and looked behind her. "These are also your relatives. They are Prophets who grandfather took care of until he died and now they need my help." She gazed back at the original Prophets. "Since you do not want my assistance, since you have aligned with someone who has nothing to lose, I am removing my hands from you. No longer will I give you money. No longer will I accept your calls. No longer will I be there when you are in need. The only exceptions to this rule are Noel, Bethany, Isabel and Samantha, because they were not involved in this betrayal. Do not try to reach out to me because I will not be accessible." She paused. "And I suggest you all find somewhere else to live. Soon."

Victory leaped up, cat hairs falling everywhere. "What do you mean find somewhere else to live?"

Nine stared into her eyes, looked down at Brett Jones and walked out, the new Prophets following.

"What does that mean?" Victory screamed to her.

When she made an attempt to follow Nine, Antonius pressed her back with a firm push to the center of her chest.

So she looked around him. "Nine, I love you! Don't do this to me! It was all Alice's fault! Please!"

****

After the meeting, Victory, Blake and Alice stepped out of the car and walked slowly toward Victory's house. Victory's jaw dropped when she approached the home she'd come to love. Just as the lawyer clarified when Nine left the meeting, every Prophet who betrayed her would need to find new places to live. Because plastered on their door was a notice to vacate the premises within sixty days.

Some years back, when his children were young adults, Kerrick purchased each of their homes in his name. He didn't keep them in his name to enact some strange power. He simply forgot to give them the titles and they forgot to ask. And as a result, each property belonging to him was rightfully Nine's because they were part of the estate. That included Alice's mother's condominium.

Victory snatched the sign off of her door, walked over to the steps and flopped down. She looked at the verbiage again, hoping it wasn't as bad as the lawyer claimed.

It was.

As she wept harder, Blake sat next to her and pulled her into a one-arm embrace. He looked up at his niece and said, "This is all your fault! I hope you're happy, Alice. Because of you, she took everything from all of us!"

Angry with Nine outwitting her again, she stepped in front of them. "I can't believe you all are blaming me for this. This is just another example of her using her power against us!"

"If you aren't to blame who else could it be?" Victory yelled gazing up at her. The sun standing behind Alice made it difficult for Victory to see her face. To see if she felt any remorse. "You should've left it alone. We might not have had it all but we had some." She lowered her head. "Noel was right. She was a good person, Alice, and you were the only one she had a problem with. If only I hadn't listened to you." She shook her head. "Now it's too late."

"So I'm to blame for you not having any money saved up also?"

"I have some money, Alice," Blake interjected.

Victory looked over at him, unaware of the secret. "You do?"

"Yeah," he exhaled. "A few hundred thousand. I put it up in case something happened."

"Why didn't you tell me?" she asked him.

Silence.

In shame, she dropped her head already knowing the answer. She spent too easily and he didn't trust her.

"Thank you so much, Blake," she said hugging him. "Thank you." For a second, relief passed between them before she focused back on her niece. "Just leave."

"But—"

"Get the fuck out of here!" he screamed.

She swallowed. "I don't have anywhere to go."

"Not our problem anymore," Victory responded.

Alice looked at her relatives once more and walked toward her car, which sat on the end of the street. Her heart was filled with so many emotions. Anger. Fear. Resentment. Guilt. She was so disappointed at not defeating Nine that it didn't dawn on her until that moment that Victory and Blake were the only people who tolerated her. Now she knew how Isabel felt when she rejected her. Without them in her life, she had nothing.

Did being an outcast still make her a Prophet?

The moment she stepped to the driver's side door, a white van pulled up alongside her. Without turning around, Alice knew what was happening. The door to the other van opened and a tall soldier stepped out and walked toward her. "Get inside," he demanded.

She thought about running but knew it was no good. It was time to pay the cost. So she turned around, and eased into the waiting van to meet her fate.

CHAPTER TWENTY-ONE

"This above all, to thine own self be true."
- William Shakespeare

Nine walked into the room she'd just given Lisa within the Prophet mansion. Things were looking up since she placed Alice where she belonged, in a special place only she had access to.

Not only had she regained control over her money, she finally realized that she was in an illegal business, which required cash on hand at all times, and that she would never be caught in a similar position again. As it stood, five million dollars in stacks of one hundred and twenty dollar bills was tucked under her house, and was secured by a safe that not even the government could open.

Nine leaned against the doorway and noticed how happy Lisa, Porter, Jeremy, Wagner, Bridget and Kerrick II appeared as they looked around Lisa's room. She'd already shown everyone else their spaces within the mansion and Lisa's was the last stop.

After pushing the windows open and looking outside, Lisa took a moment to take in the beauty of Aristocrat Hills. She turned around and placed her hand over her heart. Overwhelmed with appreciation, she ran over to Nine and wrapped her arms around her body. "You have no idea how much this means to me and my family," she said looking at her brothers, son and mother.

"We are all family," Nine smiled. "That is why you are here."

Bridget walked over to Nine and softly grabbed one of her hands. "The graciousness you're showing us by sharing your home is...I can't explain it." She was at a loss for words.

"It is a huge house. Outside of my husband and son, we do not have the need for all of the space. The only thing I ask is that you refrain from going into the basement."

"We're clear on that," Bridget said, wanting no problems.

Kerrick II pulled on Bridget's leg and she picked the two-year-old up. The baby was a light-skinned version of her grandfather.

"Aren't we, children?" Bridget asked.

They all nodded yes, no one trying to upset Nine. Especially after seeing how the others were handled at the meeting with being cut out of the fortune.

"You were the neglected one, weren't you?" Bridget asked.

Nine exhaled and suppressed the sadness that lately seemed to plague her life. "I was, before grandfather gave me this home." She looked around Lisa's room. "I spent so much time inside of it that I am still trying to find my place in the world. Amongst people."

"Kerrick spoke of you before," Lisa said. "He spoke of you as if you were the reaper coming to take him away. And now he's gone?"

"I guess a man should be careful about his predictions." She grinned slyly. "They just may come true."

"Why are you doing this?" Jeremy asked rubbing the nub of his missing arm. "You could've put us in an apartment and we would've been grateful. Why let us live here?"

"This place has over fifty different rooms. I could not live in all of them if I tried." She paused. "And I helped you because...well, because you are just like me. Thrown away like trash when all you wanted was an ounce of grandfather's love. Of anybody's love."

Nine walked deeper into the room and toward the window. She sat down on the large ledge and looked out at her vineyard.

"I helped you because I know what it is like to witness your mother love a man who could never love her in public." She crossed her arms over her chest and looked over at Bridget. "Maybe this home is the place where the broken come to be repaired. To be healed. I guess we will have to wait and see."

She looked down at the vineyard again, which secretly held Fran's body. Every drop of wine produced by the Prophets would be touched with the soil of her flesh.

"I knew my father had money but I never thought it was like this," Wagner said. "I don't know what to say."

"Well as my new uncles and aunt, the first thing we need to do is make you look like the money you possess. I am going to have my glam crew get you together and I have already made an appointment for you to get new teeth, Porter, and for you to get another prosthetic arm, Jeremy. After your appointments, you will all be taken shopping. We are Prophets and it is important that we always dress the part. We will show the others what a legitimate Prophet really looks like."

****

Nine removed the large decorative pillows off the bed with Leaf and placed them on the chaise across the room. "Why do they have to live here, Nine?"

"Not you too," she said rolling her eyes.

"What does that mean?" he asked pulling the comforter down on his side of the bed before sitting on the edge of it to remove his socks. He lay down and eased into the pocket of the covers.

"You sound like them. The Prophets who believe that just because they shared grandfather and grandmother's blood that they are purer than we are." She paused. "I will show them what it is like to be on the outside of my grace. They fucked up by coming at me and trying to take my money, and now they know." She got into bed and nestled closely next to him.

"You're like your grandfather in more than one way, Nine."

"Meaning?"

"I saw what you've been building in the house. *Finally*."

"You have not seen everything."

By T. Styles   191

"I've seen enough." He maneuvered his body so that he was lying on his side and looking into her eyes. "You have two people, including Alice, under the house. In a prison that you made. Banker is going crazy and is acting like you used to. What's going on?"

"Why would anybody be in prison? Because they deserve to be there."

"Why not kill them?" he yelled. "You're not a warden. And if you do this shit, it'll come back on you in one way or another."

"It already has," she joked.

"Do you believe in karma?"

"You have got to be kidding me, Leaf," Nine laughed. "You are speaking to the one person who lives, sleeps and breathes karma."

"And yet you choose to imprison Banker and Alice anyway." He pointed at his head. "Is there anything in your mind that realizes that shit is wrong? Don't you remember how you felt when it was done to you?"

"What about their karma? How do you know they are not getting what is due them?" She lay on her back and looked up at the ceiling. "Grandfather, imprisoned me for most of my life. And look how I turned out. I want to give them a chance to be rehabilitated."

"And if they can't?"

"Then I guess I will have to put them out of their misery."

"You've been planning this for a moment."

She giggled. "Yes, but I originally thought it would be just Alice. Which is why I allowed her to live after I warned her and she betrayed me anyway. Imagine my surprise when I found out that Banker was working with her. After I give them what they deserve, I will release them from their misery. Whether through pain or death."

****

Nine thought she was dreaming when she was suddenly awakened by Leaf's soft but panicky voice. "Nine, Nine, wake up, bae."

When she opened her eyes and turned on the lamp, she saw Isabel sitting on top of him with a knife to his throat. The tip of the blade was shivering and she was straddling his waist.

Carefully, Nine eased out of bed and tiptoed behind Isabel. Her heart thumped in her chest as she noticed that with one slash of the blade she could end her husband's life, killing Nine emotionally in the process. If ever there was a time to be cautious, now was it. "Isabel," Nine said softly, "you cannot hurt him. Please."

"But the colors are loud." She paused, moving the blade two inches closer to his throat. "He wants me like the others and no other man will have me in that way."

"Baby, I don't—"

"Shhh," Nine said placing her finger over her lips to silence him. He was liable to say the wrong thing and get himself killed.

In Isabel's erratic mental state, earlier that night she eased into bed like she always had when Leaf was gone, before they got back together. And Leaf, believing she was Nine, moved to have sex with her before realizing who she was.

His touch made Isabel snap.

When he was speechless, Nine placed her hands softly on Isabel's shoulders. She lowered her head and whispered into her ear. "Do not do this to me," she said. "Do not take him from me. I love him." She gazed down at her husband who was the most fearful she'd ever seen him.

"But he takes me in the night. He takes me in the night and makes me do all kinds of things. His fatty flesh stinks and he smells of alcohol. I can't do it anymore. I just can't!" Huge teardrops danced off of her face and splashed on his chin.

While Nine had her ear, she snaked her right hand down to her breast to take away the crazy, then she eased her hand down between her legs and onto the tip of her clit. Slowly Nine stroked it until she relaxed under the pressure of her motions.

Isabel's head drooped backwards and fell against Nine's breasts as she gave into the feelings. And when she was under her spell, Nine eased her left hand around her neck and squeezed tightly, forcing the knife out of her grasp.

Leaf leaped out of the bed and yanked Isabel from his wife's hands and tossed her on the floor. With both hands around her throat, he was about to steal her life until Nine said, "Baby, please, do not. She...she is not well. Let me get her some help."

"I don't want to hear that shit! Dr. Banning wasn't able to help you, why would I believe she's going to help her?"

"I will get her some outside help, Leaf. Please, do not do this. She is family and to kill her is to take a part of me."

Leaf looked at Nine while still squeezing Isabel's neck.

"Leaf...please," she whispered.

Finally, he released. Isabel rolled to one side and coughed several times. Tugging at the skin covering her throat, she desperately tried to snatch air back into her lungs using huge coughs.

Leaf walked up to Nine and ran his hand down the side of her face. He took a moment to look intently into her eyes. "You will no longer run this family. You will no longer make all of the decisions. I am your husband and I want this bitch out of my house. Tonight!"

"But—"

"It's either her or me!"

****

Nine was packing Isabel's bag when Lisa walked into the room. "Stormy Woods Mental Facility is ready for Izzy," she said standing in the doorway. When she saw Nine's hand shaking, she walked inside. "Let me do that for you." She removed the folded shirt from her hand and Nine flopped down on the bed.

"I wanted to help her. I really did." She paused. "I guess I thought if I helped her I would be helping myself too."

"Izzy will be fine, Nine. Trust me."

"How are you sure?"

Lisa placed a thick strand of her hair behind her ear. "I know because mama suffered from psychotic episodes for most of my childhood."

Nine looked up at her. Lisa now received her total attention. "Bridget? But she seems so relaxed."

She smiled and nodded yes.

"I guess it worked."

Lisa sighed. "It did, but she had to go away for awhile. That's when me and my brothers got extra close." She placed a pair of jeans into the suitcase and zipped it up. "And I married Wagner in a small ceremony, with just us. We always had to defend each other when she left and before we knew it we isolated ourselves from most of the world. They didn't understand us anyway." She looked ahead of her. "Daddy came by and would drop off some money to help us but I knew his heart was here. Never with us."

Nine looked over at her. "Are you in love with Wagner?"

"Yes. I love my husband. But it's hard showing people in public, who know that we're siblings. They don't understand what it means to care about someone. To care about a person so much that you see past the bloodlines. I think that makes us powerful, don't you?"

Nine nodded yes.

"All I want to do is take care of my baby and make Wagner happy, you know?" Lisa paused. "And I want to help you if you need it."

"Nine, the van is here," Antonius said knocking on the door lightly.

"Is Izzy downstairs?"

"Yes." He paused. "I have Titus with her and I told the other soldiers to go home like you requested."

Nine dismissed the others because she didn't want anyone else knowing that Isabel would be taken to a mental institution. Not even her most trusted men. She wanted to give her that privacy so that she could get well and not worry about what the men thought or felt about her. Besides, most of them had come to love Isabel and she didn't want them feeling differently, even if the vehicle transporting her was unmarked.

Nine stood up and hugged Lisa. "Thank you for sharing with me. I am glad you are here." She walked toward the door and followed Antonius downstairs.

****

Nine sat in the van in front of the Prophet mansion with Antonius after dropping off Isabel hours earlier at the mental institution. Her property seemed eerily quiet and she knew it was because one of her favorite cousins was no longer there. "Is there anything I can do for you?" Antonius asked looking into her eyes.

"No," she breathed heavily. "You have done a lot for me already, and I am grateful for you."

Before she left, he handed her something. "Keep this so that you are never alone."

She looked down at it, touched his face and slid out of the car. Antonius watched her the entire time.

The moment she walked through the door and tossed her Céline bag on the table, she stepped a few feet inside and was struck over the back of the head with a bat. She passed out cold.

CHAPTER TWENTY-TWO

"Sirs, drag them from the pit unto the prison."
- William Shakespeare

Nine lay face up on the bed, her limbs sprawled out at each end and tied to the bedposts. Naked. Gates stood at the bottom of the bed and from his view, he could see the pinkness of her center. His tongue hung out the side of his mouth as he gazed down at her flesh.

"I don't know what you did to get her so mad but you had fun with her," he said as he looked toward his right at Leaf who was tied up and sitting in a chair, his mouth bound and gagged. "And now I'm going to have a little fun too." He chuckled loudly. "I hope you don't mind me digging into the cookie jar."

Upon hearing his words, Leaf struggled to get out of the restraints and Nine's heart broke silently for him. What it must've felt like not to be able to help her. Not to be able to come to her rescue. Just like Leaf, she was gagged and was unable to say a word.

When Nine dropped Isabel off, she never realized the mistake she made by dismissing her soldiers. Without their protection, Gates was able to break into the mansion, bringing eight people with him who were able to subdue her family. He tried to enter the basement but Nine had already begun to lock it for fear her new relatives would wander downstairs and see her secret prison.

Gates, dressed in only a t-shirt and grey sweatpants, removed his clothing. With a revolver in his hand, he crawled toward her until his stiffness pushed against the opening of her vagina. He placed the gun against the tip of her nose and said, "Don't make me separate your beauty from your body." He paused. "I don't want to do you like that."

Nine closed her eyes and held her anger inside. Her body was as stiff as a corpse.

As Gates eased into her, he looked over at Leaf, loving the look of hate on his face. "I don't have to tell you why I'm doing this," he continued as he pushed deeper into Nine's center. "I think you already know but if I must, I will." His body began dripping with thick sweat. "You have to understand how hard it was for me to lose my daughter." He made his strokes long and wide with the focus being to enjoy the tightness of her body and to get revenge on Leaf at the same time. "So now I'm going to take a little pussy before—" He bit down on his bottom lip. "Oh…you have to excuse me for a minute, man. I knew this pussy was good but I never thought it would feel like this."

Gates quieted down as he continued to rape Nine roughly. Although Leaf was inflamed with anger, Nine was cool and calm. She managed to go elsewhere in her mind since she'd been physically abused before and detached from her experiences.

When he was about to reach an orgasm he said, "Damn, man, I thought I'd be able to last longer than this." He looked into Leaf's eyes before gazing down at Nine whose expression was blank as a white sheet of paper. "But when you got pussy as good as this you gotta give in to it."

At the point of ecstasy, he removed his penis and splashed his semen onto the top of her stomach. When he was emptied he wiped a little with the tip of his finger, walked over to Leaf, pulled down the gag covering his mouth and spread his nut on the top of Leaf's lip before putting the gag back in place.

Leaf went into a violent outbreak with another man's cream on his mouth and he almost freed himself until Gates stole him with a hard right, forcing him into temporary sanity.

"Calm down," he laughed. "I'm about to put you out of your misery in a minute. Soon you'll forget all about this bitch. Soon you'll forget about everything."

When he was done he walked back over to Nine and stood at the head of the bed again stroking his now limp dick. The sleekness of her body due to his sweat made her look oily, disgusting even. It was a far cry from how he perceived her since their first encounter.

"Well, Nine, I must admit, you were as good as I thought you would be but now I must let you go." He picked up the gun that sat on the edge of the bed while he raped her. "It was such a pleasure but I can't allow you or your husband to live after what you took from me.

"You probably don't know this, or even care, but because of you my wife left me and took my only remaining daughter after Dymond was murdered by Kerrick. And I know you didn't have anything to do with that, but your husband did." He looked at Leaf. "He was responsible for both of my daughters being murdered and I could not deal with him being alive. Ever. First, I wanted to take you for myself but you wouldn't go with the program. Now it's too late."

He was about to pull the trigger when Nine thrust her leg slightly to the right. It was the first movement she made since his defilement of her body and he was interested in what she was trying to say.

Instead of killing her like his mind suggested, he removed the gag from her mouth and said, "So you have a few final words after all?" He chuckled.

"Do you think your daughters had pussies wetter than mine?" she asked with a sly grin.

The smug smile disappeared from his mug when he heard her statement. "Excuse me?"

"I asked do you think your daughters had wetter pussies than me?"

Irritated, he was about to fire until she said, "What about the one daughter left? The one who is still living that was supposed to be with your wife?" She paused having gained his complete attention. "Do you know where she is, Sir Gates? Because I do."

He searched her eyes for a joke but saw none. Besides, he'd known Nine long enough to realize when she was serious and at the moment she was humorless. "What are you talking about? Where is my daughter?"

"You know, at first, when I found out who she was, I thought you sent her here for some strange reason. But after speaking to my accountant and learning that she was siphoning money from my bank accounts, a few hundred at a time, I realized she tried to get at me and Leaf on her own. That you were clueless that your daughter came here to get revenge for my husband killing her siblings." She readjusted herself as much as she could with the binds around her arms. "But she was out of her league. Wasn't she?"

His body trembled. "Are you saying that my daughter is…in this house?"

Silence.

Quickly he rushed to the head of the bed and released the ropes. Now that Leaf heard why Nine kept Banker beneath the house, everything made sense.

Gates grabbed a fistful of her hair in the back of her scalp and pushed and shoved her toward the basement, but he couldn't enter. When they made it to the door, she stared at it and then Gates. "You can kill me now if you want to but I will never tell you how to get inside unless you release my husband."

Angry at how she attempted to have the upper hand, he shoved her back toward the bedroom. Once there he placed a gun to Leaf's head. "I will fucking kill this nigga! Do you hear me? I'll fucking kill him. Is that what you want? Do you even care?"

"If you kill my husband I will die with him and still, I will never open that door." She looked into his eyes, hoping that he could feel her seriousness. "You know that what I am saying is true." She turned around and showed him her back, still chewed up from Kerrick's lashes. "And if you are considering torture, think again. I have endured it all. You can do whatever you want to me but that door will remain locked and your daughter will die a horrible death. Of starvation. The worst kind!" She paused. "Is that what you want your only child to go through?"

She looked at Gates but avoided eye contact with Leaf. Although he never said, he stood by the motto the United States held. And it was to never negotiate with terrorists.

"Do what you must, Gates," Nine said still avoiding eye contact with her husband. "I am waiting."

Seething mad, Gates placed the gun next to Leaf's head, cocked and pulled the trigger. Nine didn't move, although a urine droplet trickled down her inner thigh that they couldn't see.

When he saw how cold she was, he looked into her eyes. "You really don't care, do you?" He paused. "That explains why he was already tied up."

Nine was confused.

"Release my husband and put down your weapon, or I will not free your daughter." She paused. "On that, Sir Gates, I will not waiver."

****

Instead of freeing Leaf, Gates instructed his men to move him, still bound to the wooden chair, to the living room. But to appease Nine for the moment, he released her aunt Lisa, her uncles and their mother Bridget. Her new family members stood behind the chair Leaf sat on while Gates' men maintained their guns aimed at the family.

"Okay, I let them go. Now open this door so I can see my baby girl. If she's really here, then I'll release everyone."

Nine grabbed a device off of the floor, slid a small grey panel to the side, and placed her entire hand on the touchpad and the door leading to the basement slid open. Gates followed Nine down three flights of stairs before stopping upon a large room. She slid the panel aside and placed her palm on the pad, opening a room with a prison. Two cells were filled with Alice and Banker. However, there was no touchpad to open the cells, otherwise Gates would've killed her, cut off her hand and freed them with her cold palm.

"Nine, please let me out," Alice screamed, grabbing the bars and stuffing her face through them. "I can't stay in here anymore! I can't take the dark! It talks to me!"

Nine ignored her. What she had planned for her cousin could not be altered with words.

As Alice continued to yell, Banker's eyes fixated on her father. Slowly they moved toward each other, the thick iron bars separating them.

Beside himself with grief, he placed his hands on the bars and looked into her eyes. "Berry, what are you doing in here?" He called her by her birth name, not the fake name she adopted of Banker Troy. "I thought you were in Aruba with your mother."

"I'm sorry, daddy," she said with a low head. "I wanted to…to get them back for what they did to me. Now look." She exhaled. "I'm so sorry, daddy. I never wanted to put you through this."

Slowly he turned around and faced Nine. "What do you want?"

When he heard gun blasts upstairs, Gates knew what happened. Nine managed to alert her soldiers that there was danger using the device in her hand. The one that fell on the floor when they knocked her over the head and now his men were dead.

When Nine left Antonius earlier, he handed her the device, having no idea how he may have saved her life. After the Russians came to the property, Antonius intended to do whatever he could to protect her, so only one push of the button would let him know that she was in trouble.

Within seconds, Antonius, Leaf, and three other men from the Legion rushed down the stairs. Everyone surprised at Nine's makeshift prison and how much trouble she'd gone through to keep people incarcerated.

With guns aimed at Gates, he knew what was up. Slowly he looked down at the floor and then at Banker before placing his weapon on the ground.

He surrendered.

As he raised his hands into the air, Nine walked toward a wall directly across from him. She removed a panel, which revealed a small safe. After entering the code into the keypad, it popped open and she took out a set of keys. She removed one and handed it to Leaf. She also gave him Gates' weapon. "You can kill him or beat him. It is your choice."

Nine strolled toward the door and her men followed, before closing the door behind them.

"Get on your knees," Leaf ordered Gates.

He complied and said, "I guess there is no chance I can convince you not to kill me."

Through clenched teeth, he said, "Not a chance in hell."

"Please," Gates said, "I'm not ready to die."

"I had big plans for you, Gates, but I can work with this situation just the same. Do you remember me saying that there would come a time when you would beg me for mercy? We've come to that moment."

Gates in that second knew that his pleas were of no use.

He was going to die.

"I dreamed about this moment," Leaf continued as he looked down at him. "When you and I would be alone." He walked around Gates' body before stopping behind him. He peered down at the center of his head. "I imagined choking you, or stabbing you until I saw your eyes roll behind your head."

"Please don't kill my father," Banker whispered from behind the cell bars.

"Shut the fuck up, bitch!" he yelled pointing at her.

She backed up into the cell and sat down on the bed.

"And now I realize you aren't worth it."

Gates laughed and slowly shook his head from left to right. "You know what's wrong with you Prophets? Besides the fact that you fuck each other? You honestly believe that you are the only ones entitled to revenge. Like you're the only ones who hurt or feel pain!" He paused. "You took two of my daughters away from me!" he cried. "Two of them! If the shoe was on the other foot, and it had been your family, you would've taken me out a long time ago!"

"You're right," Leaf nodded. "But you didn't take me out. Instead, you waited and sneakily tried to steal my wife. Then you raped her in front of my face." He brought the butt of the gun down on the side of his head, splitting it in the process. "Say what you want, I would've never done no shit like that! You made me a monster." He paused. "And after all this, I'm still going to show you mercy." He exhaled, looked up at the ceiling and placed the gun to the top of his head.

Pow!

****

Leaf walked up the stairs leading to the living room and flopped down on the recliner across from the sofa were Nine was sitting. *Waiting.* His clothing and hand were sprinkled with blood. "Where is everyone else?"

"They went to get liquor," she shrugged. "Only one week in this house and look what happened. I guess they needed a drink so Antonius took them to the store."

Leaf chuckled softly although he didn't find a lot funny. Seeing Nine being raped, having another man's cum on his face and committing murder in one day did something deplorable to his psyche.

"How did it go?" she asked.

"He dead."

"But I heard two shots."

"I let his daughter go with him."

She nodded, although that was not her plan. She wanted to play with Banker a bit longer. "Well at least this was done quietly, without the winery getting involved."

Leaf gazed over at her. "What is up with you and that wine shit?"

"I—"

"You what?" he yelled, causing his temples to throb. "Don't give a fuck about nothing but that shit!"

"It is not that I—"

"I'm sick of you and that wine," he continued, cutting her off. "You make me want to—"

"IT WAS MY FAULT SHE WAS KILLED!" Nine yelled, her body trembling.

The bass of her voice caused Leaf to pause.

In a low whisper, she said, "It was my fault." Her head hung low. "Had she not been trying to teach me to be strong, to be safe, grandfather would have never killed her and I have never been able to forgive myself for it." She wept. "So I...so I wanted to do this so that her name would live on. So that she would always know how much I love her." Nine wiped the tears from her face and sighed. "I just want her to know that I love her."

He leaned back in the chair, the warm gun still in his grasp. "What about me? Do you love me?"

"Must you ask?"

"Then why were you going to let him kill me upstairs?"

She averted her gaze toward the floor. "Is that what you believe?" She looked at him. "Or is that what you want to believe?"

"I want the truth."

"I was not going to allow him to kill you." She paused. "I would have stopped it way before that happened."

"And when were you going to do that? When he pulled the trigger the second time?"

She smiled. "When he was on top of me, forcing himself into my body, I saw the chamber of his gun. The first one did not have a bullet inside of it, Leaf. So he could not have killed you."

He exhaled, relieved to hear that at least she had a plan. "Why didn't you tell me?"

"How could I? It would have ruined everything!"

Leaf laid back, his face bludgeoned. "What I don't know, what I can't understand is why he sent the old lady first. Why did Gates have her and her henchman tie me to the chair?"

Nine's eyebrows squished together. "What old lady?"

"I was downstairs, by the backdoor when you took Isabel to the institution. I guess somebody left the door open and this big white man hit me over the back of the head with a blunt object. I still don't know what it was." He paused. "But when I came to, I was tied to the chair."

Nine's mind swirled. That's what Gates meant about him already being tied up. "What were they saying?"

"Nothing really. Just kept asking me about you and telling me I would be rewarded." Leaf searched his mind but considering the events of the day, everything seemed cloudy. "She used the word Goddess too." He touched his head. "I don't know, bae. It's foggy."

"Dr. Banning is on her way," she said. "Do not worry about it. It is obvious that they were with Gates and must have left before I came back. I just hate that they got away before we could do something about it."

He closed his eyes and his mind wandered to another thought. "We'll see them again. I'm sure. She's an old lady. How bad can she be? Baby, is Antonius in love with you?"

"Yes," she whispered. "Why do you ask?"

"Because he seems to know when you need him. He seems to always be there. How do you know that he wasn't involved in all of this? To get you to depend on him?"

"How do we know anything, husband? How do we know who is capable of what at any given time? For now, all I know is that he saved me. He saved us. I also know that he was loyal when I needed him most. That is all I can ask."

"You finally called me husband."

"Because you are."

Silence.

"But there is something else," Nine said.

Frustrated, Leaf placed the gun in his lap and looked into the ceiling. Wiping his hands down his face, he sighed and said, "What now, bae?"

"Gene had a son who is staying with Antonius for the moment. I am worried for the child, Leaf. He is such a sweet little boy and if he is put into the system, we will lose him for good. He may turn out like his father or worse. Let me help him. It is not like we do not have the money. He needs to be around a man like you. Will you raise him? And love him like you do Julius?"

"What are you saying really?"

"I am asking if it is okay that we take him into our home."

He smiled and shook his head. He never realized he married a woman with such a strong need to help others until then. "And if I say no?"

Deflated, she said, "Then he would have to go somewhere else. And I would have to love him from afar."

He smiled having heard the right words. "Okay, let's do it."

She stood up, rushed over to him and plopped on his lap. "There is something else."

He placed the gun on the table beside him. "Nine, please!" he yelled. "What is it now?"

"I am pregnant."

He didn't know whether to laugh or be mad at how she manipulated the situation. She was real smart about getting him to say yes to letting Denarius stay with them first, because had he known, he would've said they should focus on their own child. "Are you serious, bae?"

"Yes," she nodded. "Can you believe after all of this, the Phenethylamine poison and the madness, that I am going to have our baby?"

He rubbed her back, and felt an immense sense of pride. "It's the only good that has happened in all of this."

"I love you, husband."

"You just talking shit," he chuckled.

She reached into the back pocket of her jeans and pulled out a white sheet of paper. It was a legal document she had the lawyer draw up during all the madness with her banking accounts. "What is this?"

"Read it."

He opened the document and what he saw made him love her all over again. It was a name change. She was now Nine Lincoln.

"You know you don't have to do this, right?" He paused trying not to appear too excited, only to lose his cool, although his light skin was flushed red from blushing. "Through all this shit, I realized I am what I am and you are what you are."

"What do you mean?"

"The beef with the Prophets was my father's thing. Not mine. So I'm going to adopt the name I should've had all along. From here on out, I will be known as Leaf Prophet."

She laughed. "So I got this done for nothing?"

"No, not for nothing," he said moving her chin so that she was looking into his eyes. "I'll know that you did this for me, despite what the world calls you. What the world calls us. And that means more to me than anything."

"We are Prophets," she said proudly.

"I guess we are."

EPILOGUE
CHRISTMAS EVE

A huge spectacular white Christmas tree sat in the corner of the Prophet mansion in the living room as Nine, Leaf, Bridget, Lisa, Wagner, Jeremy and Porter decorated it with bulbs and tinsel.

Everyone except Nine, who was pregnant, sipped Francesca wine, while Denarius and little Kerrick II kept Julius company by making funny faces at him, as he sat in the playpen.

The Bose speakers embedded in the wall played The Whispers' version of "This Christmas" and for the first time in a long time, Nine felt as if she were a part of something real. Her home was filled with family members who at one point or another had been forgotten. And she felt proud that she was able to bring them together.

As Nine decorated the fireplace, Leaf walked up behind her while she was hanging a stocking. He placed his warm lips against her ear and said, "You sure you have to go? We could always go upstairs and do our thing."

His voice vibrated through her body, causing her to tingle all over. Smiling, she said, "Unfortunately, I do, husband." She sighed, "I have not seen her since she left some months back. I want her to know that she still has family. And I need to make sure she is okay."

He didn't like the idea of her leaving at night but he knew how she felt about Isabel and would not stand in the way. Just as long as she didn't bring her into their home. That was one promise Nine made to him that he would never allow her to take back. "Who's going with you?"

She turned around and placed her arms around his waist. Looking up into his eyes, she said, "I am going inside alone."

He rubbed her shoulders. "Is that right? You're not even taking your most prized possession? The great Antonius?"

"I need protection," she said touching her belly. "Especially since I am pregnant with your child." She paused. "I would have taken you but you hate her. Do not worry, though, he will remain in the car."

"It's not that I hate Isabel," he said. "I just wonder about her, that's all. Don't forget she put a knife to my neck, Nine. I have a right not to be in her fan club." He kissed her nose.

"But she is still your cousin."

"And I don't know her like that." He paused. "Speaking of cousins, what about the one downstairs?" he whispered not wanting to alert the others.

"Why are you so concerned with what I do in my leisure time?"

He gripped her arms and pulled her to him. His warm breath fell upon her face. "What you are doing is wrong, Nine. What have you turned in to? You don't hold people against their will just because you can."

"Have you forgotten how she tried to steal my money? And ruin me? What if you had not found them? I would be broke!" She paused. "Besides, confinement is not that bad. It was done to me."

Silence.

He released her and said, "Are you feeding her today? Since it is Christmas Eve?"

Angry he was so concerned with her, she clenched her jaw and pushed away from him. Moving toward a plate with turkey, stuffing and cranberry sauce, she said, "I am already on it."

Although she assumed nobody was interested in what went down in the basement, she underestimated Lisa, who was always looking, listening and watching. Despite the rules, she was going to enter that basement and learn its secrets, if it was the last thing she did.

Once downstairs, Nine walked to a private room, across from the prison. Opening the door, she looked ahead, at the painting on the wall that once belonged to Gates. She always coveted the painting that was done by a young artist named Antoinette Bateau. It resembled a bleeding vagina and Nine wondered what Antoinette's mind frame was when she created it.

After looking at the painting, she opened the door to the prison and approached Alice's cell. Her cousin's once confident mien disappeared a long time ago and was replaced with something Nine could not recognize. Although confined, there was something right beneath the surface of her soul that refused to be shattered and Nine hated her for it.

Nine strolled casually up to the cell, slid the plate under the bars and sat down in a chair in front of it. Alice crawled over to the plate and snatched the food off of it as if she were a dog.

When she was done, she stood up and with a mouthful of food and said, "I don't know why you're looking at me like I'm a science project, Nine."

"You are a disgrace," Nine laughed. "It is funny how no one, not even your mother, bothered to ask about you. All they want to do is get me to change my mind about cutting them off. To show me how much they care. It is all about the money."

Alice's eyes began to water. "I don't care about them. I don't care about no one and I will never be who you want me to be."

Nine smiled. "Yes you will. Everyone can be broken."

"Why do you say that? Because you shattered so easily under my pressure?" she asked slyly.

Nine's foot fidgeted. "You do not know what you are talking about, inmate. It would be wise if you learned your place instead of biting the hand that feeds you."

"I know exactly what I'm saying," she giggled. "At one time, you were virtuous and even though I hated you, I respected you for being the same. For knowing who you were. But now, well now you're just like me. A person who was born to hate and who loves it."

There was visible tension in Nine's shoulders and arms. "I am nothing like you, Alice Prophet!" she yelled standing up.

"Oh?" she said sarcastically. "Is that why you get pleasure off of seeing me behind this wall?"

By T. Styles 211

"I gave you a chance to do what was right!" She pointed at her. "I warned you of what would happen if you went against me and you did it anyway."

Alice laughed heartedly. "You didn't give me a chance to do anything but what you knew I would! You knew I wouldn't accept your meaningless offer. You expected me to do exactly what I did, go against you with all my might. That way you would feel validated in keeping me here."

"I brought you here to teach you a lesson!"

"You aren't keeping me here to teach me a lesson. Or even to punish me. You're keeping me here because you enjoy having a prisoner. Tell the truth and be free, Nine! You were angry when Leaf killed Banker, weren't you? Because you would've had two playthings." She laughed. "You enjoy having a toy so that you can go upstairs and fuck your own cousin. My presence gives you orgasms at night." She laughed. "Doesn't it, Nine Prophet?" Alice's thin face spewed words of fire and Nine trembled upon hearing what she recognized as truth.

"You have made me angry beyond reset, Alice. On Christmas day, I am going to snatch out your eyes." Alice's smile dematerialized. "Let us find out if you see the world the same way then."

She moved for the exit.

Alice placed her hands on the bars and stuffed her thin face between them. "You're just like me, Nine Prophet!" she yelled as Nine moved through the door. "Do you hear me? Just like me!"

****

Nine followed a pretty white nurse down the hallway to visit her cousin in Stormy Woods Mental Facility. Although it was not her intent, Alice had placed her in a bad mood and she was hoping to release the negative energy.

Before she approached Isabel's room, her phone rang. It was Leaf. "Bae, you gotta come home right away!"

"I just got to the center. I cannot leave right now." She paused. "What is wrong?"

"There's a religious protest out in front of our house! It's on the news and everything!"

"A protest, for what?"

"For who we are," he said in a deep voice. "But guess who's leading the charge."

"Who?"

"The woman who was in our house. The one I thought was with Gates. I recognized her face!"

"I am confused." She rubbed her temples.

"Me too. But her name is Sister Anna Marie Cartwright. They're calling us abominations and everything."

Nine stumbled a little.

"Are you alright?" the nurse asked placing a hand on her shoulder.

"I am fine," she lied.

The nurse removed her hand and stepped a few feet back to give her some privacy.

All this time, Nine had no idea that the woman, who had been in her home on the night Gates was killed, was Anna. Leaf had lost so much blood that some of his memory went with it. For a week, she questioned him endlessly about the woman's description but he kept saying it was dark and that he could not see or remember much.

Anna was determined to extort money from Nine. When her original plan to use Joshua did not work, since he resigned his position at the shelter and went into hiding after speaking to his niece Isabel, she tried to get at Nine through Leaf. But Gates had his own plans that night. So Anna and her goons left the Prophet mansion with haste, leaving Leaf beaten and tied up in their wake.

With no other recourse, Anna decided to expose the Prophets, like she had done in the past with the senator and Pope, secretly hoping to be paid off by Nine finally.

"Leaf, I will be home when I can," she said.

"Call me when you get on the property. I'm going to have some of the men try to clear the road up so you'll be safe. Baby, you should see the people's faces. They fucking hate us! I have a feeling shit is not going to be the same for our family after this."

"Me too."

After ending the call with Leaf, she was shaken up but had to go on with the visit so that she could get home quickly. "She's in that room right over here." The nurse pointed at a large metal door with a window.

Confused, she said, "I cannot walk in and talk to her?"

"Not now. It's too early for Isabel to have contact. Besides, she must learn to follow the rules." She walked away.

Slowly Nine approached the door and peered in. Everything was white but it still felt dark inside. Isabel was sitting in the classic Prophet position, on the floor, back against the wall and knees to her chest. Her eyes were closed and her soft hair had grown like weeds around her braids, causing them to dread up. "Isabel," Nine whispered. "Can you hear me?"

Upon perceiving Nine's voice, she rose up, and approached the door. With wide eyes and a huge smile, she said, "Cousin, are you coming to take me home?"

Nine's chin dipped toward her chest. "Not right now," she said regretfully. "They tell me you are not ready, so we have to follow the rules."

"The rules?" Isabel frowned. "Since when does Nine Prophet follow rules?" She walked away and sat on the edge of her thin bed. "I made one mistake, Nine. I made one mistake and for that I deserve to be punished for life?" She paused. "You know that I'm not crazy. You've had long lucid conversations with me. Don't you remember?"

"But you also tried to kill my husband and jump off of a banister. I just want you well, Isabel. That is all."

She rolled her eyes. "You said I was like you. Is this how you would treat yourself?"

Silence.

Nine lowered her head. "Just follow the program, Izzy. Follow the program and I will get you out of here."

"Do you know what they consider following the program to be in this place? To take a bunch of pills every hour," she cried. "They want to steal my spirit, Nine," she said touching her chest, "but they can't have it! It's not up for sale or negotiation! I won't let them!"

"Isabel, just—"

"Go away, Nine Prophet! I'm hearing loud colors again. And even behind these doors, I can still attack."

Needing to take care of matters at home, Nine backed away. Her walk was slow at first before turning brisk. She was almost out of the wing when she heard, "Nine, is that you?"

The sound of the woman's voice sent chills down her body, stopping her at once. How could it be possible? She was told she was dead. Slowly she moved toward the sound of the voice and when she did, she was staring into her birth mother's eyes.

She was looking at Kelly Prophet.

TIMELINE OF BIRTHS
The Original PROPHETS

1953 – Kerrick is born

1976 – Kelly is born

1977 – 2nd CHILD – Avery is born

1978 – 3rd CHILD – Marina is born

1979 – 4th CHILD – Victory is born

1980 – 5th CHILD – Justin is born

1992 – Kelly and Avery's Child – Lydia is born. (Killed by a car)

- Paige is born. (Murdered later by Nine)

1993 – Marina and Joshua Saint's Child – Alice is born.

1994 – Victory and Blake's Child – Noel is born.

1995 – Victory and Blake's Child – Samantha is born.

1996 - Victory and Blake's Child - Isabel is born.

1997 – Victory and Blake's Child – Bethany is born.

1997 – Kelly and Avery's Child - Karen is born. (Deformed. Murdered by Kerrick.)

- Corrine and Justin's Child – Autumn (Leaf) is born.

1998 – Kelly and Avery's Child - Nine is Born.

2014 – CURRENT

TIMELINE OF BIRTHS
The Illegitimate PROPHETS

1992 – Kerrick and Bridget's Child - Lisa is born.

1993 – Kerrick and Bridget's Triplets – Wagner, Porter and Jeremy are born.

2012 – Lisa and Wagner's Child – Kerrick II is born.

CHARACTERS FROM OTHER CARTEL PUBLICATIONS NOVELS

BAMBI & THE KENNEDY KINGS – From the *PRETTY KINGS* series

YVETTE, MERCEDES, CARISSA and **LIL C** – From the *PITBULLS IN A SKIRT* series

KELSI – From the book *A HUSTLER'S SON 2*

RASIM and **SNOW NAMI** – From the book *PRISON THRONE*

The Cartel Publications Order Form
www.thecartelpublications.com
Inmates **ONLY** receive novels for $10.00 per book.

Shyt List 1		$15.00
Shyt List 2		$15.00
Shyt List 3		$15.00
Shyt List 4		$15.00
Shyt List 5		$15.00
Pitbulls In A Skirt		$15.00
Pitbulls In A Skirt 2		$15.00
Pitbulls In A Skirt 3		$15.00
Pitbulls In A Skirt 4		$15.00
Victoria's Secret		$15.00
Poison 1		$15.00
Poison 2		$15.00
Hell Razor Honeys		$15.00
Hell Razor Honeys 2		$15.00
A Hustler's Son 2		$15.00
Black and Ugly As Ever		$15.00
Year Of The Crackmom		$15.00
Deadheads		$15.00
The Face That Launched A		$15.00
Thousand Bullets		
The Unusual Suspects		$15.00
Miss Wayne & The Queens of DC		$15.00
Paid In Blood (eBook Only)		$15.00
Raunchy		$15.00
Raunchy 2		$15.00
Raunchy 3		$15.00
Mad Maxxx		$15.00
Quita's Dayscare Center		$15.00
Quita's Dayscare Center 2		$15.00
Pretty Kings		$15.00
Pretty Kings 2		$15.00
Pretty Kings 3		$15.00
Silence Of The Nine		$15.00
Silence Of The Nine 2		$15.00
Prison Throne		$15.00
Drunk & Hot Girls		$15.00
Hersband Material		$15.00
The End: How To Write A		$15.00
Bestselling Novel In 30 Days (Non-Fiction Guide)		
Upscale Kittens		$15.00
Wake & Bake Boys		$15.00
Young & Dumb		$15.00

By T. Styles

Young & Dumb 2: _____ $15.00

Tranny 911 _____ $15.00
Tranny 911: Dixie's Rise _____ $15.00
First Comes Love, Then Comes Murder_____ $15.00
Luxury Tax _____ $15.00
The Lying King _____ $15.00
Crazy Kind Of Love _____ $15.00

Please add $4.00 **PER BOOK** for shipping and handling.

The Cartel Publications * P.O. BOX 486 OWINGS MILLS MD 21117

Name:
_____
Address:
_____
City/State:
_____
Contact# & Email:
_____

Please allow 5-7 BUSINESS days before shipping. The Cartel is **NOT** *responsible for prison orders rejected.*

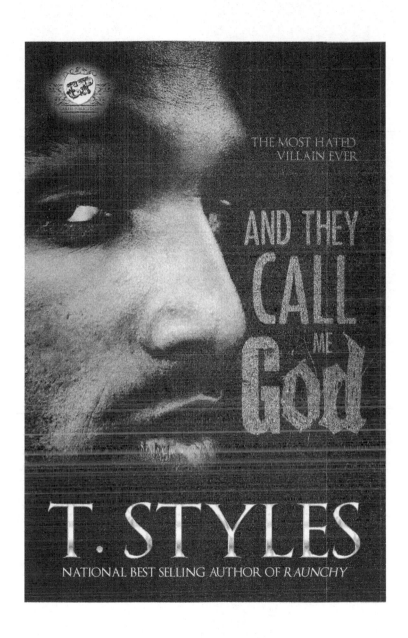

THE MOST HATED
VILLAIN EVER

AND THEY
CALL
ME
God

T. STYLES

NATIONAL BEST SELLING AUTHOR OF *RAUNCHY*

By T. Styles

CPSIA information can be obtained
at www.ICGtesting.com
Printed in the USA
LVOW03s1452080218
565809LV00001B/230/P